Praise for *Silverview*

"[Le Carré] was often considered one of the finest novelists, period, since World War II. It's not that he 'transcended the genre,' as the tired saying goes; it's that he elevated the level of play. . . . [*Silverview's*] sense of moral ambivalence remains exquisitely calibrated."
—*The New York Times Book Review*

"The plot unfolds with as much cryptic cunning as a reader could want. . . . Enjoyable throughout, written with grace, and a welcome gift from the past."
—*The Wall Street Journal*

"A thoroughly enjoyable book . . . A clarion call that slices straight to the bone, and hurts. John le Carré did not just leave the world an engaging novel, he also left us with a warning." —*The Washington Post*

"This is an intelligent, mournful, wry delight. . . . A suitable end to a storied career, a low-key thriller with a brain and a conscience."
—*Star Tribune*

"What a gift to have a posthumous novel by John le Carré, a writer who gave us a world of intricate spycraft, government mendacity and corrupt capitalist overlords that was as unromantic as it was immersive and transporting."
—*Vogue*

"*Silverview* is a propulsive and elegantly written tale . . . a fully formed thriller that provides a stinging look at the British Secret Service operating under crisis. . . . [It] has all the grand themes of his best novels—love and betrayal, loyalty and morality—fully on display."
—*AARP*

"A well-aimed parting shot."
—*The New Republic*

"A worthy coda . . . from a much-missed master." —*The Economist*

"One of [le Carré's] most touching and satisfying [novels]—for putting into high relief this beloved author's vision for his country and his disappointments, and perhaps most of all, the elegance and coloristic palette of his unique and incomparable prose."
—*Pittsburgh Post-Gazette*

"*Silverview* is a fine book centered on the lonely lives of spies and [the] difficult choices they make when experience redefines the parameters of their mission for Queen and country. . . . John le Carré at the top of his game—smart, candid, stylish, relevant." —*Valdosta Daily Times*

"First-rate prose and a fascinating plot distinguish the final novel from MWA Grand Master le Carré. . . . This is a fitting coda to a remarkable career." —*Publishers Weekly*

Praise for John le Carré

"The premier spy novelist of his time. Perhaps of all time." —*Time*

"[Le Carré's] novels are so brilliant because they're emotionally and psychologically absolutely true." —*The New York Times Book Review*

"Le Carré is one of the best novelists—of any kind—we have."
—*Vanity Fair*

"No other writer has charted—pitilessly for politicians but thrillingly for readers—the public and secret histories of his times."
—*The Guardian* (London)

PENGUIN BOOKS

SILVERVIEW

John le Carré was born in 1931. For six decades he wrote novels that came to define our age. The son of a con man, he spent his childhood between boarding school and the London underworld. At sixteen he found refuge at the university of Bern, then later at Oxford. A spell of teaching at Eton led him to a short career in British Intelligence, in MI5 and MI6. He published his debut novel, *Call for the Dead*, in 1961 while still a secret servant. His third novel, *The Spy Who Came in from the Cold*, secured him a worldwide reputation, which was consolidated by the acclaim for his trilogy: *Tinker, Tailor, Soldier, Spy*; *The Honourable Schoolboy*; and *Smiley's People*. At the end of the Cold War, le Carré widened his scope to explore an international landscape including the arms trade and the War on Terror. His memoir, *The Pigeon Tunnel*, was published in 2016 and the last George Smiley novel, *A Legacy of Spies*, appeared in 2017. *Silverview* is his twenty-sixth novel. John le Carré died on December 12, 2020.

Silverview

JOHN LE CARRÉ

PENGUIN BOOKS

PENGUIN BOOKS
An imprint of Penguin Random House LLC
penguinrandomhouse.com

First published in the United States of America by Viking, an imprint of
Penguin Random House LLC, 2021
Published in Penguin Books 2022

Chapters 2 and 4 first published in slightly different
form in *Harper's Magazine*, September 2021.

ISBN 9780593490631 (paperback)

THE LIBRARY OF CONGRESS HAS CATALOGED THE HARDCOVER EDITION AS FOLLOWS:
Names: Le Carré, John, 1931–2020, author.
Title: Silverview / John Le Carré.
Description: [New York] : Viking, [2021]
Identifiers: LCCN 2021037129 (print) | LCCN 2021037130 (ebook) |
ISBN 9780593490594 (hardcover) | ISBN 9780593490600 (ebook)
Subjects: LCGFT: Novels.
Classification: LCC PR6062.E33 S47 2021 (print) | LCC PR6062.E33 (ebook) |
DDC 823/.914—dc23
LC record available at https://lccn.loc.gov/2021037129
LC ebook record available at https://lccn.loc.gov/2021037130

Printed in the United States of America
1   3   5   7   9   10   8   6   4   2

Set in Dante MT Std

Silverview

I

At ten o'clock of a rainswept morning in London's West End, a young woman in a baggy anorak, a woollen scarf pulled up around her head, strode resolutely into the storm that was roaring down South Audley Street. Her name was Lily and she was in a state of emotional anxiety which at moments turned to outrage. With one mittened hand she shielded her eyes from the rain while she glowered at door numbers, and with the other steered a plastic-covered push-chair that contained Sam, her two-year-old son. Some houses were so grand they had no numbers at all. Others had numbers but belonged to the wrong street.

Arriving at a pretentious doorway with its number painted with unusual clarity on one pillar, she climbed the steps backwards, hauling the pushchair after her, scowled at a list of names beside the owners' bell buttons, and jabbed the lowest.

'Just give the door a push, dear,' a kindly woman's voice advised her over the speaker.

'I need Proctor. She said Proctor or no one,' Lily said, straight back.

'Stewart's on his way now, dear,' the same soothing voice announced, and seconds later the front door opened to reveal a stalky, bespectacled man in his mid-fifties, with a leftward lean to his body, and a long beakish head tilted in semi-humorous enquiry. A matronly woman with white hair and a cardigan stood at his shoulder.

'I'm Proctor. D'you want a hand with that?' he asked, peering into the pushchair.

'How do I know it's you?' Lily demanded in reply.

'Because your revered mother phoned me last night on my private number and urged me to be here.'

'She said alone,' Lily objected, scowling at the matronly woman.

'Marie looks after the house. She's also happy to lend any kind of spare hand if needed,' said Proctor.

The matronly woman stepped forward but Lily shrugged her away, and Proctor closed the door after her. In the quiet of the entrance hall she rolled back the plastic cover until the top of the sleeping boy's head was revealed. His hair was black and curly, his expression enviably content.

'He was awake all night,' Lily said, laying a hand on the child's brow.

'Beautiful,' the woman Marie said.

Steering the pushchair under the staircase where it was darkest, Lily delved in its underside and extracted a large unmarked white envelope and stood herself before Proctor. His half-smile reminded her of an elderly priest she'd been supposed to confess her sins to at boarding school. She hadn't liked the school and she hadn't like the priest and she didn't intend to like Proctor now.

'I'm supposed to sit here and wait while you read it,' she informed him.

'Of course you are,' Proctor agreed pleasantly, peering crookedly down at her through his spectacles. 'And can I also say, I'm very, very sorry?'

'If you've got a message back, I'm to give it to her by mouth,' she said. 'She doesn't want phone calls, texts or emails. Not from the Service or anyone. Including you.'

'That's all very sad too,' Proctor commented after a moment of sombre reflection, and, as if only now waking to the envelope he was holding in his hand, he poked at it speculatively with his bony fingers: 'Quite an opus, I must say. How many pages, would you think?'

'I don't know.'

'Home stationery?' – still poking – 'Can't be. Nobody has home stationery this size. Just normal typing paper, I suppose.'

'I haven't seen inside. I told you.'

'Of course you did. Well' – with a comic little smile that momentarily disarmed her – 'to work, then. Looks as if I'm in for a long read. Will you excuse me if I withdraw?'

In a barren sitting room on the other side of the entrance hall Lily and Marie sat facing each other in lumpy tartan chairs with wooden arms. On a scratched glass table between them lay a tin tray with a Thermos of coffee and chocolate digestive biscuits. Lily had rejected both.

'So how is she?' Marie asked.

'As well as can be expected, thanks. When you're dying.'

'Yes, it's all awful, of course. It always is. But in her spirit, how is she?'

'She's got her marbles, if that's what you mean. Doesn't do morphine, doesn't hold with it. Comes down for supper when she can manage.'

'And still enjoys her food, I hope?'

Unable to take more of this, Lily marched to the hall and busied herself with Sam until Proctor appeared. His room was smaller than the first and darker, with grubby net curtains, very thick. Concerned to preserve a respectful distance between them, Proctor positioned himself next to a radiator on the far wall. Lily didn't like the set of his face. You're the oncologist at Ipswich Hospital, and what you're about to say is for close family only. You're going to tell me she's dying, but I know that, so what's left?

'I'm taking it for granted that you know what your mother's letter says,' Proctor began flatly, no longer sounding like the priest she wouldn't confess to, but somebody a lot more real. And seeing her brace herself for denial: 'Its general thrust anyway, if not its actual contents.'

'I told you already,' Lily retorted roughly. 'Not its general thrust or anything else. Mum didn't tell me and I didn't ask.'

It's the game we used to play in the dormitory: how long can you stare out the other girl without blinking or smiling?

'All right, Lily, let's look at it another way,' Proctor suggested with infuriating forbearance. 'You don't know what's in the letter. You don't know what it's about. But you've told this or that friend that you were popping up to London to deliver it. So who've you told? Because we really need to know.'

'I have not told one single fucking word to anybody,' Lily

said, straight into the expressionless face across the room. 'Mum said don't, so I didn't.'

'Lily.'

'What?'

'I know very little of your personal circumstances. But the little I do know tells me you must have a partner of some sort. What did you say to him? Or if it's a her, to her? You can't simply vanish from your stricken household for a day without offering an excuse of some kind. What more human than to say, quite by the way, to a boyfriend, girl-friend, pal – even to some casual acquaintance – "Guess what? I'm popping up to London to hand-deliver a super-secret letter for my mother"?'

'You're telling me that's human? For us? To talk like that to each other? To a casual acquaintance? What's human is, Mum said she didn't want me to tell a living soul, so I didn't. Plus I'm indoctrinated. By your lot. I'm signed up. Three years ago they held a pistol to my head and told me I was grown up enough to keep a secret. Plus I haven't got a part-ner, and I haven't got a bunch of girlie friends I bubble to.'

The staring game again.

'And I didn't tell my father either, if that's what you're asking,' she added, in a tone that sounded more like a confession.

'Did your mother stipulate that you shouldn't tell him?' Proctor enquired, rather more sharply.

'She didn't say I should, so I didn't. That's us. That's our household. We tiptoe round each other. Maybe your house-hold does the same.'

'So tell me, then, if you will,' Proctor went on, leaving

aside what his family did or didn't do. 'Just for interest. What ostensible reason did you give for popping up to London today?'

'You mean what's my cover story?'

The gaunt face across the room brightened.

'Yes, I suppose I do,' Proctor conceded, as if cover story were a new concept to him, and a rather jolly one at that.

'We're looking at a nursery school in our area. Near my pad in Bloomsbury. To get Sam on the list for when he's three.'

'Admirable. And will you actually be doing that? Looking at a real school? You and Sam? Meet the staff and so on? Get his name down?' – Proctor the concerned uncle now, and a pretty convincing one.

'Depends how Sam is when I can get him out of here.'

'Do please manage it if you can,' Proctor urged. 'It makes it so much easier when you get back.'

'Easier? What's easier?' – bridling again – 'You mean easier to lie?'

'I mean easier not to lie,' Proctor corrected her earnestly. 'If you say you and Sam are going to visit a school and you visit it, and you then go home and say you've visited it, where's the lie? You're under quite enough strain as it is. I can barely imagine how you put up with it all.'

For a discomfiting moment, she knew he meant it.

'So the question remains,' Proctor continued, returning to business, 'what reply should I ask you to take back to your extremely brave mama? Because she's owed one. And must have it.'

He paused as if hoping for a little help from her. Receiving none, he went on.

'And, as you said, it can only be by mouth. And you will have to administer it alone. Lily, I'm really sorry. May I begin?' He began anyway. 'Our answer is an immediate yes to everything. So three yesses in all. Her message has been taken to heart. Her concerns will be acted upon. All her conditions will be met in full. Can you remember all that?'

'I can do the little words.'

'And, of course, a very big thank you to her for her courage and loyalty. And for yours too, Lily. Again. I'm so sorry.'

'And my dad? What am I supposed to tell him?' Lily demanded, unappeased.

That comic smile, yet again, like a warning light.

'Yes, him. You can tell him all about the nursery school you're going to visit, can't you? After all, it's why you came up to London today.'

*

With raindrops spitting up at her from the pavement, Lily kept going as far as Mount Street, where she hailed a cab and ordered the driver to take her to Liverpool Street Station. Maybe she'd really meant to visit the school. She no longer knew. Maybe she'd announced as much last night, although she doubted it, because by then she'd decided she was never again going to explain herself to anyone. Or maybe the idea hadn't come to her till Proctor squeezed it out of her. The only thing she knew was: she wasn't going to visit any bloody school for Proctor's sake. To hell with that, and dying mothers and their secrets, and all of it.

2

On the same morning, in a small seaside town perched on the outer shores of East Anglia, a 33-year-old bookseller named Julian Lawndsley emerged from the side door of his brand new shop and, clutching to his throat the velvet collars of a black overcoat left over from the City life he had renounced two months previously, set off to battle his way along the desolate seafront of shingle beach in search of the one café that served breakfast at this dismal time of year.

His mood was not friendly, either towards himself or the world at large. Last night, after hours of solitary stocktaking, he had climbed the stairs to his newly converted attic flat above the shop to discover he had neither electric power nor running water. The builder's phone was on answer. Rather than take a hotel room, if one was even to be found at that time of year, he lit four kitchen candles, uncorked a bottle of red wine, poured himself a large glass, piled spare blankets on the bed, got into it and buried himself in the shop's accounts.

They told him nothing he didn't know. His impulsive

escape from the rat-race had got off to a wretched start. And if the accounts didn't say the rest of it, he could say it for himself: he was not equipped for the loneliness of celibacy; the clamorous voices of his recent past were not to be quelled by distance; and his lack of the basic literary education required of your upmarket bookseller was not to be repaired in a couple of months.

The one café was a clapboard shack squeezed behind a row of Edwardian beach huts under a blackened sky packed with screaming seabirds. He had seen the place on his morning runs, but the thought of entering it had never crossed his mind. A faulty green sign flickered with the word ICE minus its s. Forcing the door open, he held it against the wind, entered and eased it back into place.

'Good morning, my dear!' yelled a hearty female voice from the direction of the kitchen. 'You seat you anywhere! I come soon, okay?'

'And good morning to you,' he called vaguely in return.

Under fluorescent lights lay a dozen empty tables covered in red plastic gingham. He chose one and cautiously extracted the menu from a cluster of cruets and sauce bottles. The babble of a foreign news announcer issued through the open kitchen door. A crash and a shuffle of heavy feet from behind him informed him of the advent of another guest. Glancing at the wall mirror, he was guardedly amused to recognise the egregious person of Mr Edward Avon, his importunate but engaging customer of the previous evening, if a customer who had bought nothing.

Though he had yet to see his face – Avon, with his air

of perpetual motion, being far too preoccupied with hanging up his broad-brimmed Homburg hat and adjusting his dripping fawn raincoat over the back of a chair – there was no mistaking the rebellious mop of white hair or the unexpectedly delicate fingers as, with a defiant flourish, they extracted a folded copy of the *Guardian* newspaper from the recesses of the raincoat and flattened it on the table before him.

*

It is yesterday evening, five minutes to closing time. The shop is empty. It has been empty for most of the day. Julian is standing at the till, totting up the day's meagre takings. For some minutes he has been aware of a solitary figure in a Homburg hat and fawn raincoat, armed with a furled umbrella, standing on the opposite pavement. After six weeks of running a stagnant business, he has become quite the connoisseur of people who stare at the shop and don't come in, and they are beginning to get on his nerves.

Is it the shop's pea-green paintwork the man's disapproving of – he's an old inhabitant maybe, and doesn't like garish? Is it the many fine books on display, special offers to suit all pockets? Or is it Bella, Julian's twenty-year-old Slovakian trainee, frequently to be found occupying the shop window in search of her various love-interests? It is not. Bella is for once gainfully employed in the stockroom, packing unsold books to be returned to their publishers. And now – miracle of miracles – the man is actually making his way across the street, he is removing his hat, the shop door is opening, and a sixty-something face under a mop of white hair is peering round it at Julian.

'You're shut,' an assured voice informs him. 'You're shut, and I shall come another time, I insist' – but already one muddy brown walking shoe is inside the door, and the other is easing its way after it, followed by the umbrella.

'Not shut at all, actually,' Julian assures him, matching smooth for smooth. 'Technically, we close at five thirty, but we're flexible, so please just come in and take all the time you need' – and, with this, resumes his counting while the stranger studiously threads his umbrella into the Victorian umbrella stand and hangs his Homburg on the Victorian hat stand, thereby paying his respects to the shop's retro-style, selected to appeal to the older age group, of which the town has a plentiful supply.

'Looking for something particular or just browsing?' Julian asks, turning up the bookshelf lights to full. But his customer barely hears this question. His broad, clean-shaven face, mobile as any actor's, is alight with marvel.

'I'd absolutely no idea at all,' he protests, indicating with a flowing gesture of his arm the source of all his wonderment. 'The town may boast a real-life bookshop at last. I am amazed, I must say. Totally.'

His position now manifest, he sets off on a reverential inspection of the shelves – fiction, non-fiction, local interest, travel, classical, religion, art, poetry – here and there pausing to fish down a volume and subject it to some kind of bibliophile's test: front cover, inside flap, quality of paper, binding, general weight and friendliness.

'I must say,' he exclaims again.

Is the voice entirely English? It's rich, interesting and compelling. But is there not a very slight foreign flavour in the cadence?

'You must say what?' Julian calls back from his tiny office, where he is now running through the day's emails. The stranger begins again, on a different and more confiding note.

'Look here. I'm assuming that your magnificent new shop is under entirely different management. Am I right, or am I barking up the completely wrong tree?'

'New management is right' – still from his office, through the open doorway. And, yes, there is a foreign flavour. Just.

'New ownership also, one may ask?'

'One may, and the answer is emphatically yes,' Julian agrees cheerfully, taking up his former position beside the till.

'Then are you – forgive me.' He starts again, severely, on a more military note: 'Look here – are you by any chance, or are you not, the young mariner himself, because I need to know? Or are you his deputy? His surrogate. His whatever?' And then, arbitrarily concluding, with some reason, that Julian is offended by these searching questions: 'I mean absolutely nothing personal, I assure you. I mean only that, whereas your undistinguished predecessor christened his emporium the Ancient Mariner, you, sir, as his more youthful and may I say vastly more acceptable successor –'

By which time, the two of them are in a silly all-English tangle, until everything is properly patched up, with Julian confessing that, yes, indeed, he is both manager and owner, and the stranger saying, 'Mind awfully if I help myself to one of these?' and deftly winkling a get-to-know-us card from its housing with his long pointy fingers, and holding it to the light to scrutinise the evidence with his own eyes.

'So I am addressing, correct me if I'm wrong, Mr J. J. Lawndsley in person, sole owner and manager of Lawndsley's Better Books,' he concludes, lowering his arm with theatrical slowness. 'Fact or fiction?' – then swinging round to observe Julian's response.

'Fact,' Julian confirms.

'And the first J, if one may make so bold?'

'One may, and it's Julian.'

'A great Roman emperor. And the second – even bolder?'

'Jeremy.'

'But not the other way round?'

'Never on any account.'

'Does one call you Jay-Jay?'

'Personally, I recommend plain Julian.'

The stranger ponders this with knitted brows, which are prominent and gingery, and flecked with white.

"Then, sir, you are Julian Lawndsley, not his portrait, not his shadow, and I for my sins am Edward Avon, like the river. I may be Ted or Teddy to the many, but to my peers I am Edward all alone. How d'you do, Julian?' – thrusting a hand across the counter, the grip surprisingly powerful, despite the fine fingers.

'Well, hullo, Edward,' Julian replies jauntily and, withdrawing his hand as soon as he is decently able, waits while Edward Avon makes a show of deliberating his next move.

'Will you permit me, Julian, to say something personal and potentially offensive?'

'As long as it's not too personal,' Julian replies warily, but in a similarly light vein.

'Then would you mind frightfully if, with all due diffidence, one made an absolutely footling recommendation regarding your extremely impressive new stock?'

'As many as you like,' Julian replies hospitably, as the danger cloud recedes.

'It is a totally personal judgement and merely reflects my own feelings on the matter. Is that clearly understood?' Evidently it is. 'Then I shall proceed. It is my considered view that no local interest shelf in this magnificent county, or in any other county for that matter, should regard itself as complete without Sebald's *Rings of Saturn*. But I see you are not familiar with Sebald.'

See from what, Julian wonders, even as he concedes that the name is indeed new to him, and all the more so since Edward Avon has used the German pronunciation, *Zaybult*.

'*Rings of Saturn*, I must warn you in advance, is not a guidebook as you and I might understand the term. I'm being pompous. Will you forgive me?'

He will.

'*Rings of Saturn* is a literary sleight of hand of the first water. *Rings of Saturn* is a spiritual journey that takes off from the marches of East Anglia and embraces the entire cultural heritage of Europe, even unto death. Sebald, W. G.' – this time using the English pronunciation and waiting while Julian writes it down. 'Formerly Professor of European Literature at our University of East Anglia, a depressive like the best of us, now, alas, dead. Weep for Sebald.'

'I will,' Julian promises, still writing.

'I have overstayed my welcome, sir. I have purchased nothing, I am good for nothing, and I am in awe. Goodnight, sir. Goodnight, Julian. All good fortune with your superb new enterprise – but wait! Is that a basement I see?'

Edward Avon's eye has lighted on a descending spiral staircase tucked into the further corner of the Reduced to Clear department, and partly concealed by a Victorian screen.

'Empty, I'm afraid,' Julian says, returning to his takings.

'But empty for what purpose, Julian? In a bookshop? There must be no empty spaces, surely!'

'Still thinking about it, actually. Maybe a second hand department. We'll see' – beginning to tire.

'I may take a look?' Edward Avon insists. 'Out of shameless curiosity? You allow?'

What can Julian do but allow?

'Light switch on your left as you go down. Watch your step.'

With a nimbleness that takes Julian by surprise, Edward Avon vanishes down the spiral staircase. Julian listens, waits, hears nothing and puzzles at himself. Why did I let him do that? The man's as mad as a flute.

As nimbly as he has vanished, Avon reappears.

'Magnificent,' he declares reverently. 'A chamber of future delights. I congratulate you unreservedly. Goodnight, once more.'

'So may I ask what you do?' Julian calls after him as he starts towards the door.

'I, sir?'

'You, sir. Are you a writer yourself? An artist? A journalist? An academic. I should know, I'm sure, but I'm new here.'

The question appears to puzzle Edward Avon as much as it does Julian.

'Well,' he replies, having apparently given the matter much thought. 'Let us say I am a British mongrel, retired, a former academic of no merit and one of life's odd-job men. Will that do you?'

'I guess it will have to.'

'I bid you anon, then,' Edward Avon declares, casting him a last wistful look from the door.

'And anon to you,' Julian calls cheerfully back.

At which Edward Avon-like-the-river dons his Homburg hat, adjusts its angle and, umbrella in hand, sweeps bravely into the night. But not before Julian has been subjected to the heavy aroma of alcoholic fumes on his departing breath.

*

'You decide what you wanna eat today, my dear?' the proprietor was asking Julian in the same strong mid-European accent with which she had greeted his arrival. But before he could answer, it was Edward Avon's rich voice that was resounding over the boom of the sea wind and the creaks and groans of the café's flimsy walls:

'Good morning to you, Julian. You rested soundly amid

the turmoil, I trust? I suggest you go for one of Adrianna's bumper omelettes. She does them remarkably well.'

'Oh, right. Thanks,' Julian returned, not yet quite willing to use the Edward. 'I'll give it a shot.' And to the ample waitress standing at his shoulder: 'With brown toast and a pot of tea, please.'

'You want fluffy, like I make Edvard?'

'Fluffy's fine.' And, to Avon, resignedly: 'So is this a favourite watering-hole of yours?'

'When the urge takes me. Adrianna is one of our little town's best-kept secrets, aren't you, darling?'

The insistent voice, for all its verbal flourishes, struck Julian as a trifle underpowered this morning, as well it might be, if last night's breath was anything to go by.

Adrianna clumped happily back to the kitchen. An uneasy truce reigned, while the sea wind howled and the gimcrack building heaved under the stress and Edward Avon studied his *Guardian* newspaper, while Julian had to content himself with staring at the rainswept window.

'Julian?'

'Yes, Edward?'

'A most amazing coincidence, actually. I was a friend of your late lamented father.'

Another crash of rain followed.

'Oh, really? How extraordinary,' Julian replied, at his most English.

'We were incarcerated in the same appalling public school together. Henry Kenneth Lawndsley. But to his school friends fondly known as the great H. K.'

'He often said his schooldays were the happiest of his life,' Julian conceded, not at all convinced.

'And, alas, if one surveys the poor fellow's life, one might sadly conclude that he was speaking no less than the truth,' said Avon.

And after that, nothing except the crashing of the wind again, and the foreign gabble of the radio from the kitchen, and Julian discovering an urgent need to get back to the empty bookshop where he didn't yet belong.

'I suppose one might,' he agreed dully, and was grateful to see Adrianna approaching with the fluffy omelette and his tea.

'You allow I join you?'

Whether Julian allowed or not, Avon had already risen to his feet, coffee in hand, leaving Julian not knowing which to be more surprised by: the man's evident familiarity with his father's unfortunate life, or Avon's reddened eyes sunk into their sockets, cheeks cracked with pain-lines and coated in silvery stubble. If this was last night's hangover, the man must have been on the bender of a lifetime.

'So did your dear father ever mention me?' he asked when he had sat down, leaning forward and appealing to Julian with his haggard brown eyes. 'Avon? Teddy Avon?'

Not that Julian remembered. Sorry.

'The Patricians Club? He didn't speak of the Patricians to you?'

'He did. Yes, he did,' Julian exclaimed, the last of his doubts for better or worse receding. 'The debating club that never was. Set up by my father and banned after half a meeting. He nearly got slung out for it. As he tells it – or did,' he added cautiously, since his late father's accounts of himself did not always stand the test of accuracy.

'H. K. was Club Chairman, I was his Vice. They nearly threw me out too. I very much wish they had' – swig of cold black coffee – 'Anarchists, Bolsheviks, Trotskyites: whatever doctrine enraged the Establishment, we hastened to adopt it.'

'That's pretty much how he described it too,' Julian acknowledged, then waited, as Avon did, each for the other to play the next card.

'And then, oh dear, your father went up to Oxford,' Avon recalled at length, with a stage shudder, and a lowering of the underpowered voice, and a clown's lift of the bushy eyebrows to Heaven, followed by a sideways glance at Julian to see how he was responding, 'where he fell into the hands' – placing his own hand on Julian's forearm in sympathy – 'but perhaps you are of a religious disposition, Julian?'

'I'm not,' Julian replied emphatically, his anger rising.

'I may go on, then?'

Julian went on for him:

'Where my father fell into the hands of a bunch of American-financed born-again evangelical mind-benders with short hair and smart ties who carted him off to a Swiss mountaintop and turned him into a fire-breathing Christian. Is that what you wanted to say?'

'Perhaps not in such harsh language, but I could not have put it better. And you are truly not religiously disposed?'

'Truly not.'

'Then you have the foundations of wisdom within your

grasp. There he was at Oxford, poor man, "as happy as Larry", as he wrote to me, his whole life before him, girls galore – yes, they were his weakness, and why not? – and, by the end of his second year –'

'They'd got him, okay?' Julian cut in. 'And ten years after he'd been ordained into the holy Anglican Church, he recanted his faith from the pulpit in front of his whole Sunday flock: I, the Reverend H. K. Lawndsley, Clerk in Holy Orders, do hereby declare that God does not exist, Amen. Is that what you were going to say?'

Was Edward Avon proposing they now dwell on his father's prolific sex life and other dissipations, as widely aired in the gutter press of the day? Was he pressing for the gory details of how the once-proud Lawndsley family was turfed out of its vicarage into the street without a penny? And how Julian himself, in the wake of his father's premature death, had to dump his hopes of university and become a runner in a City trading house owned by a remote uncle, in order to pay off his father's debts and put bread on his mother's table? Because, if he were, Julian was going to be out of the door in twenty seconds cold.

But Edward Avon's expression, far from salacious curiosity, was the very mask of heartfelt sympathy.

'And you were there, Julian?'

'Where?'

'In the church?'

'As it happened, yes, I was. Where were you?'

'I wished only to be at his side. As soon as I read what had happened to him – a little late, alas – I wrote to him post-haste, offering whatever inadequate help I could. The hand of friendship, such money as I had.'

Julian allowed himself time to consider this.

'You wrote to him,' he repeated, in a questioning tone, as the shades of his earlier disbelief returned. 'And did you ever get an answer?'

'I received none and I deserved none. On the last occasion your father and I met, I had called him a Holy Fool. I could hardly take it amiss when he spurned my offer. We have no right to insult another man's faith, however absurd it is. You agree?'

'Probably.'

'Naturally, when H. K. renounced his faith I was filled with pride for him. As indeed vicariously, dare I say it, I am filled with pride for you, Julian.'

'You are what?' Julian exclaimed, laughing out loud despite himself. 'You mean because I'm H. K.'s son and I've opened a bookshop?'

But Edward Avon found nothing to laugh at.

'Because, like your dear father, you found the courage to defect: he from God and you from Mammon.'

'What's that supposed to mean?'

'I understand you were a highly successful trader in the City.'

'Who told you that?' Julian demanded stubbornly.

'Last night after leaving your shop, I prevailed on Celia to allow me to use her computer. Immediately, all was revealed, to my enormous sadness. Your poor father, dead at fifty, one son, Julian Jeremy.'

'Celia your wife?'

'Celia of Celia's Bygones, your distinguished neighbour in the high street and collecting point for our overgrowing population of rich weekenders from London.'

'Why did you have to go sneaking off to Celia's? Why didn't you just come out with it in the shop?'

'I was divided. As you would be. I hoped, but I was uncertain.'

'You were also pretty refreshed, if I recall.'

Avon appeared not to hear this:

'I was immediately drawn by the name. I knew only too well there had been a scandal. I had no idea how the drama had played out, nor of your poor father's death. If you were H. K.'s son, I could imagine how you had suffered.'

'And my supposed defection from the City?' Julian asked, refusing to be appeased.

'Celia happened to mention that you had abandoned a lucrative livelihood in the City at no notice, and she was appropriately mystified.'

Julian would have liked very much at this point to return to the little matter of Edward Avon's claim to have offered his father the earth in his hour of need, but Edward Avon had other ideas. He had rallied remarkably. There was a new zeal in his eyes. His voice had recovered its flowery richness:

'Julian. In the name of your dear father. And since Providence has twice brought us together in the space of a few hours. Concerning your large and beautiful basement. Have you considered what treasures it might contain, what a work of miracle it might be?'

'Well, no, as a matter of fact, I don't think I quite have, Edward,' Julian replied. 'Have you?'

'I have thought of little else since we met.'

'Glad to hear it,' Julian said, not without scepticism.

'Suppose you created – in that splendid space, still virgin – something so untried, so alluring and original, as to be the talking point of every literate and would-be-literate customer in the area?'

'Suppose.'

'Not a mere second hand books department. Not an arbitrary book depository of no character, but a purposefully selected shrine to the most challenging minds of our time – and of all time. A place where a man or woman may come off the street knowing nothing, and leave enlarged, enriched and craving more. Why do you smile?'

A place where a fellow who has recently declared himself a bookseller, and only afterwards realised that such a vocation has its own queer skills and knowledge, might blamelessly and invisibly acquire them, while appearing all the while to provide them from his own stock to a grateful public.

But, even as the unworthy thought occurred to him, Julian was starting to believe in the idea for its own sake. Not that he was yet prepared to acknowledge that to Edward Avon.

'You were sounding a bit like my father for a moment. I'm sorry. Go on.'

'Not just the great novelists, who are obvious. But philosophers, free-thinkers, founders of great movements, even those we may abhor. Chosen not by the dead hand of the ruling cultural bureaucracy, but by Lawndsley's even Better Books. And called –'

'Called what, for instance?' Julian demanded, off balance.

Avon paused, the further to arouse his audience's expectation:

'We shall call it the Republic of Literature,' he declared, and sat back with his arms folded while he studied his man.

And the truth was that, even if Julian had started out thinking this the most overblown sales pitch he had ever been subjected to, one that played with suspicious accuracy upon his sense of cultural deficit – not to mention an outrageous presumption on the part of a man whose bona fides he continued strenuously to question – nevertheless Edward Avon's grand vision spoke straight to his heart, and to the reason he was here at all.

Republic of Literature?

He bought it.

It rang bells.

It was classy, but had universal appeal. Go for it.

And he might have offered a more encouraging reply than his City man's kneejerk of 'Sounds pretty good, I'll have to think about it', had not Edward Avon already been on his feet, gathering up his Homburg hat and fawn raincoat and umbrella on his way to the counter, where he now stood deep in conversation with the abundant Adrianna.

But in what language were they conversing?

To Julian's ear it was the language of the announcer on the kitchen radio. Edward Avon spoke it; Adrianna laughed and spoke it back. Edward rallied and laughed along with her all the way to the door. Then he turned to Julian and gave him a last exhausted smile.

'I am a little down at the moment. I trust you will forgive me. So good to meet H. K.'s son. Extraordinary.'

'I didn't notice anything. I thought you were great, actually. I mean about the Republic of Literature. I was thinking you might drop by and give me the odd bit of advice.'

'I?'

'Why not?'

If a man knows his Sebald, is an academic of some sort, loves books and has time on his hands, why not indeed?

'I'm opening a coffee bar above the shop,' Julian went on engagingly. 'It'll be ready next week with luck. Come in and graze, and we can have a talk.'

'My dear fellow, what a generous offer. I shall give it my best endeavours.'

With wings of white hair streaming from under his Homburg, Edward Avon once more set off into the storm, while Julian headed for the cash desk.

'You not like your omelette, my dear?'

'Loved it. It was just a bit much. Tell me something, please. What language were you two speaking just now?'

'With Edvard?'

'Yes. With Edvard.'

'Polish, my dear. Edvard is good Polish boy. You not know this?'

No. He didn't.

'Sure. He very sad now. Got sick wife. She gonna die soon. You not know that?'

'I'm new here,' he explained.

'My Kiril is nurse. He work Ipswich General. He tell me. She don't speak Edvard no more. She chuck him out.'

'His wife chucked him out?'

'Maybe she wanna die alone. Some peoples, they do that. They just wanna die, go to Heaven maybe.'

'Is his wife Polish?'

'No, my dear.' Hearty laugh. 'She English lady' – laying a finger lengthways under her nose to indicate superiority. 'You wanna take your change?'

'It's fine. It's yours. Thank you. Great omelette.'

*

Safely back in his shop, Julian suffers a severe reaction. He had known a few con-artists in his time, but, if Edward were another, he was in a class of his own. Was it conceivable, even, that he'd been hanging around in the downpour at eight o'clock this morning – just on the off-chance that Julian would come out of the shop – then followed him to Adrianna's café for the express purpose of putting the arm on him? Was Avon, by any chance, that huddled figure he'd spotted, sheltering under an umbrella in a doorway down the street?

But what on earth was the endgame?

And if the worst Avon wanted was company, didn't Julian have a duty to provide it to his late father's old school friend, and all the more so if his dying wife had chucked him out?

And the clincher – how could Edward Avon or anyone else have known that Julian's water and electricity had been turned off?

Ashamed of his unworthy thoughts, Julian makes amends by haranguing a succession of errant tradesmen on the phone, then takes to his computer and visits the site of his late father's West Country public school, currently mired in a child abuse investigation.

He confirms that an AVON, Ted (*sic*), is on record as a 'late entry scholar' to the school's sixth form. Period of attendance, one year.

He next embarks on a succession of abortive searches, first for plain Edward Avon, then for Edward Avon, academic, then for Edvard Avon, Polish speaker. He finds no plausible match.

The local telephone listings offer no Avon of any kind. He tries an online address service: number withheld.

At midday, builders appear unannounced and remain till mid-afternoon. Normal services are restored. Come evening, he leafs through his predecessor's outstanding orders for rare and second hand books, and chances on a dog-eared card marked AVON, no initial, no address, no number.

The said AVON, male or female, is interested in any hardback work in decent condition by one Chomsky, N. Probably some obscure fellow Pole, he tells himself dismissively, and is about to toss the card away when he relents and searches for Chomsky, N.:

Noam Chomsky, author of over one hundred books. Analytical philosopher, cognitive scientist, logician, public activist, critic of US state capitalism and foreign policy, repeatedly jailed. Rated world's top intellectual and father of modern linguists.

Chastened, he retires to bed after the usual solitary supper in his resurrected kitchen and finds he is unable to think consistently about any subject other than Edward or Edvard

Avon. So far, he reckons, he has met two irreconcilable versions of the man. He wonders how many more there are to come.

Falling asleep at last, he speculates whether he has discovered in himself a secret need for another father figure. He decides that one has been quite enough, thank you.

3

It was the great day, the day of days, the day that Stewart Proctor and his wife, Ellen, had been looking forward to all month: the twenty-first birthday of their twin children, Jack and Katie, which by an act of divine intervention had fallen on a Saturday. Three generations of Proctors, from 87-year-old Uncle Ben down to three-month-old nephew, Timothy, had converged upon Stewart and Ellen's large, sensible, secluded house and grounds in the Berkshire hills.

The Proctor family would never have described itself as upper class. Even the word 'Establishment' raised hackles. And entitled was quite as bad as élite. The family was liberal, southern English, progressive, devoted to endeavour and white. It was principled and committed. It was engaged at all levels of society. Its money was held in trusts and not discussed. For its education, it sent its brightest to Winchester, its second brightest to Marlborough, and a few here and there, where need or principle dictated, to state school. When polling days came round, there were no Conservative voters. Or if there were, they took good care not to say so.

On present count the Proctors could point to two learned judges, two Queen's Counsellors, three physicians, one broadsheet editor, no politicians, thank God, and a healthy crop of spies. An uncle of Stewart had been Visa Officer in Lisbon throughout the war, and we all knew what that meant. During the early days of the Cold War, the family bad apple had raised a disastrous rebel army in Albania and got a medal for it.

As to its womenfolk, back in the day there had scarcely been a female Proctor who wasn't cloistered at Bletchley Park or Wormwood Scrubs. Like all families of its kind, the Proctors knew from birth that the spiritual sanctum of Britain's ruling classes was its secret services. The awareness, never explicitly spoken of, conferred an extra solidarity on them.

With Stewart, unless you were crass, you didn't ask what he did. Or why, at fifty-five, after spending a quarter of a century either at the Foreign Office in London or in a succession of diplomatic outposts, he wasn't an ambassador somewhere, or a permanent under-secretary of something, or Sir Stewart.

But you knew.

This then was the family that was assembled that sunny spring Saturday to drink Pimm's and Prosecco and play silly games and celebrate the double birthday of the twins. Both Jack, third-year Biology, and Katie, third-year Eng. Lit., had contrived to slip away from their respective universities, and by Friday evening were in the kitchen helping their mother, Ellen, marinate chicken wings, prepare lamb racks, fetch charcoal and sacks of ice, always making sure she had a gin and tonic at her elbow, because, although no kind of alcoholic, she swore she couldn't cook without a stiff one at the ready.

Only the croquet lawn had remained by Stewart's decree un-mown, awaiting his return from London on the seven twenty p.m. from Paddington. But, with the last of daylight going, Jack took the executive decision to mow it himself, because there was trouble at mill as the family liked to say, and Stewart would have to spend the night in the flat in Dolphin Square, before catching the sparrowfart express – another family term – next morning.

So there was a bit of tension about whether he'd make it at all, or whether the trouble at mill would keep him tied up in London, until – oh bliss! – prompt at nine on the Saturday morning, there came the old green Volvo chugging up the hill from Hungerford Station, with an unshaven Stewart grinning and waving at the wheel like a racing driver, and Ellen upstairs running a bath for him, and Katie yelling, 'He's here, Mum!' and rushing to put on bacon and eggs, and her mother yelling back, 'Give the poor man a chance, for the Lord's sake!' For Ellen was old Irish, and never more so than when there was a happy crisis to celebrate.

And now at last everything was happening in real time: rock music blasting out at gale force over the relay that Jack had lashed up from the drawing room; dancing on the deck beside the spartan swimming pool – Proctors don't heat their pools – boule in the twins' old sandpit, children's six-a-side croquet, and Jack and Katie and their university pals being efficient with the barbecue, and Ellen after her labours looking leisurely and beautiful in a long dress and cardigan, and a floppy straw hat over her famous auburn hair, stretched out in a deck chair like a dowager; and Stewart periodically slipping away to his den in the old scullery at the back of the house to talk into his ultra-secure green phone, but choosing his words all the same and using as few of them as possible; then to reappear a few minutes later, the same attentive, self-effacing, jolly host they knew him for, always a word for this old aunt or that new neighbour, spotting the Pimm's glass that urgently needs refilling, or deftly removing an empty bottle of Prosecco that somebody's about to trip over.

And, come the chill of evening, with only close family and significant others remaining, it's Stewart who, after another quick visit to the old scullery, settles to the Bechstein in the drawing room for his traditional birthday rendering of the Flanders and Swann Hippopotamus song; and for an encore Noël Coward's exhortation to Mrs Worthington – On my knees, Mrs Worthington, please, Mrs Worthington – not to put her daughter on the stage.

And the young sing along, and the sweet scent of marijuana mysteriously enters the air, and at first Stewart and Ellen affect not to notice, then discover they are both dog-tired, and with a 'Bedtime for us Olds, will you forgive us?' go upstairs to bed.

*

'So what the hell's going on, Stewart, tell me?' Ellen enquires amiably enough in her rapid Irish brogue, speaking into her vanity mirror. 'You've been a cat on hot bricks ever since you came home this morning.'

'I've been nothing of the kind,' Proctor protests. 'I was the life and soul of the party. Never sang better in my life. Half an hour talking to your dear Aunt Meghan and thrashed Jack at croquet. What more d'you want?'

With studied deliberation, Ellen removes her diamond earrings, first unscrewing the keeper behind each ear, then putting them in their satin-lined box, and the box into the left hand drawer of her dressing table.

'And you're on hot bricks now, look at you. You're not even undressed.'

'I've a call coming in at eleven on the green phone and I'm damned if I'll traipse through the house in dressing gown and slippers in front of the young. It makes me feel about ninety.'

'So are we all to be blown up? Is it one of those again?' Ellen demands.

'It's probably nothing at all. You know me. I'm paid to worry.'

'Well, I certainly hope they're paying you one hell of a lot, Stewart. Because I've not seen you half as bad as this since Buenos Aires.'

Buenos Aires, where he had served as Deputy Head of Station in the run-up to the Falklands War, with Ellen as his covert number two. Ellen, ex-Trinity, Dublin, is also ex-Service, which, as far as Proctor and half the Service is concerned, is the only sort of partner to have.

'We're not about to go to war again, if that's what you're hoping,' he says, keeping up the banter, if banter it is.

Ellen offers a cheek to the mirror, dabs cleanser on it.

'Is it yet another Domestic Security case you've got on your hands?'

'It is.'

'Can you not tell me about it, or is it one of those?'

'It is one of those. Sorry.'

The other cheek.

'And is it a woman you're after, at all? You've your woman look about you, anybody can tell.'

After twenty-five years of marriage, Proctor never ceases to marvel at Ellen's psychic leaps.

'Since you ask, yes, it is a woman.'

'Is she Service at all?'

'Pass.'

'Is she ex-Service?'

'Pass.'

'Is she anybody we know at all?'

'Pass.'

'Did you sleep with her?'

Not in all their years of marriage has she asked him such a question. Why tonight? And why just one week before she embarks on a long-planned tour of Turkey under the auspices of her ridiculously handsome young archaeology tutor from Reading University?

'Not as far as I remember,' he replies airily. 'From what I hear, the lady in the case only sleeps with the First XI.'

Cheap and too close to the truth. Shouldn't have said it. Ellen unpins her incomparable auburn hair and lets it cascade over her bare shoulders, as practised by beautiful women since the beginning of time.

'Well, mind you watch out for yourself, Stewart,' she warns her reflection. 'Will you be taking the sparrowfart in the morning?'

'Looks as though I'll have to.'

'Maybe I'll tell the children it's a Cobra meeting. It'll give them a buzz.'

'But it's not a Cobra, for heaven's sake, Ellen,' Proctor protests uselessly.

Ellen detects a blemish under one eye, pats it with a cotton pad.

'And you'll not be lurking down there in the scullery all night, I trust, Stewart? Because it's a crying waste of a woman's life otherwise. And a man's.'

With sounds of jubilation issuing from every corridor, Proctor makes his way through the house to the old scullery. The green phone sits on a red plinth like a Post Office letter box. Five years ago when it was installed, Ellen in a whimsical moment had popped a tea cosy over it to keep it warm. It had been there ever since.

4

The week that follows Julian's dual encounter with Edward Avon does not lack for distractions.

A next door neighbour's underhand planning application threatens to rob the stockroom of its only source of daylight.

Returning one evening from a conference of local librarians, he is met, not by Bella, but by a locked shop and a flowered thank-you card on the till, declaring her undying love for a Dutch fisherman.

And in the precious basement, now firmly established in Julian's mind as the future home of the Republic of Literature, rising damp is diagnosed.

Yet, for all these calamities, he never ceases to reflect on the many faces of his late father's school friend. Too often he fancies Edward's raincoated shadow sweeping past the shop window without a turn of the Homburg hat. So why doesn't the wretched man come in and graze? No obligation to buy, Edward, Edvard, or whoever you are.

The more he thinks about Edward's grand plan, the more it grows on him. But does the name still ring right? Is it perhaps too high-hat after all? Might Readers' Republic have greater crowd appeal? Might Republic of Readers or New Republic of Readers, or how about Lawndsley's Republic of Readers? Or how about taking it right down and just calling it Literary Republic?

Telling no one – since there was no Edward to tell – Julian makes a dedicated journey to the print shop in Ipswich and has them run up a few tentative drafts for a full page ad in the local rag. Edward's first title is still the best.

None of which in any way prevents him, in his low moments, from taking Edward to task for his intrusive theories regarding his father and himself:

I defected from the City? Utter balls. I was a wide-awake predator from day one, and no kind of believer. I came, I stole, I conquered, I got out. End of story.

As to my lamented father: maybe – just possibly – H. K. was some kind of religious defector. When you've screwed half the pious ladies of your parish, maybe you and God do decide to call it a day.

And what about that heart-warming offer of friendship, money and whatever else that Edward Avon had purportedly made to his old pal H. K. in the hour of his distress? All Julian could say was: next time we meet, prove it.

Because whatever else you might say about the Reverend H. K. Lawndsley (retired hurt), when it came to hoarding useless junk, he was in a class of his own. Nothing was too humble to be stored away for his future, non-existent biographers: no sermon note, no unpaid bill or letter – be it from a discarded mistress, an outraged husband, tradesman or bishop – escaped his egomaniacal net.

And hidden here and there amid the mountain of dross, yes, the rare letter from a friend he'd managed to keep. And one or two of them did indeed offer assistance of a sort. But from his old school pal Edward, Edvard, Ted or Teddy, not a peep.

And it is in part this inconsistency, coupled with a great impatience to get the Republic of Literature up and running once the rising damp was fixed, that prompts Julian to set aside whatever scruples he has, and call on his fellow toiler in the high street vineyard, Miss Celia Merridew of Celia's Bygones, on the pretext of discussing the revival of the town's defunct arts festival.

*

She was waiting for him on her doorstep, feet astride, and sixty if a day, smoking a cigarillo in the unlikely sunshine. Her choice of costume was a kimono of parrot-green and orange, her ample bosom adorned with strings of brilliant beads, her hennaed hair knotted in a bun and held in place by Japanese combs.

'Not one penny, young Mr Julian,' she warned him jovially as he advanced on her. And when he assured her that it was only her moral support he was after: 'Wrong address, darling. No morals worth a bean. Come into my parlour and have a ginny.'

A hand-scrawled notice on the glass front door read FREE CAT-NEUTERING HERE. Her parlour was an ill-smelling back room of broken furniture, dusty clocks and stuffed owls. From an ancient refrigerator, she extracted a silver teapot with the price label dangling from its handle, and poured a gin concoction into two Victorian rummers. Her hate-object of the day was the new supermarket.

'They'll do you in, and they'll do me in,' she predicted in her rich Lancashire growl. 'That's all the buggers care about: putting us honest traders out of business. Soon as they spot you earning half a living, they'll open an industrial-sized book department, and won't rest till you're a charity shop. All right, let's have it about your festival. I've heard about bumble bees that fly as shouldn't. I've not heard about dead ones as can.'

Julian made his pitch, by now a practised performance. He was thinking of getting together an informal working party to explore options, he said. Might Celia agree to adorn it?

'I'll want my Bernard along to hold my hand,' she warned.

Bernard, her consort: market gardener, Freemason, part-time estate agent and Chairman of the local council's Planning Committee. Julian assured her that Bernard's presence would be a boon.

Random small talk while Celia gets the measure of him and he lets her. What about that Jones the greengrocer, then, standing for Mayor when everybody except his wife knows he's put his fancy lady in the family way? And those affordable houses they're putting up behind the church, there: whoever's going to be able to afford one of them by the time the estate agents and lawyers have taken their cut?

'So we're a public schoolboy, are we, darling?' Celia asked, appreciatively running her sharp little eyes over him. 'Went to Eton, I expect, same as the government.'

No, Celia. State.

'Well, you speak posh enough, I will say. Same as my Bernard. And I expect you've got yourself a nice girlfriend too, haven't you?' – continuing her unabashed appraisal of him.

Not at present, Celia, no. Resting, let's say.

'But the girls are what we like best, are they, darling?'

Definitely what he liked best, he agreed – but he was careful all the same, as she leaned suggestively forward to top up his ginny, not to sound overenthusiastic.

'Only I've heard a thing or two about you, you see, young Mr Lawndsley. More than I'm letting on, if I'm truthful, which I like to be. Quite the demon trader, you were. A leader in his field is what I heard. And more friends than what he has enemies, which they tell me is unusual in the City, it being cut-throat. How's custom, darling, or should I not speak ill of the dead?' she rattled on, with a saucy lift of the long skirts, and a crossing of the legs, and a sip of ginny.

Which was Julian's opportunity, by way of a couple of detours to confuse the scent, to arrive by supposed chance on the amusing topic of this oddball customer who'd barged into his shop at closing time, having had a drink or three, inspected it from top to bottom, kept Julian talking for half an hour, not bought a single book and turned out to be – he needed go no further:

'That's my Teddy, darling!' Celia cried in mock indignation. 'Over the moon he was! Came straight in here to look it all up in the computer, bless him. Oh, but when he knew your dad had passed away – what with the troubles he's got already – oh dear, oh dear,' she added, shaking her head in what Julian took to be a combined reference to his late father and Edward's ailing wife.

'My poor, poor Teddy,' she went on, as her beady eyes came back to inspect him yet again. And with barely a pause: 'You've not had any dealings with him at all, have you, darling, while you were being a City mogul?' she enquired with elaborate innocence. 'Direct or indirect, as we might say? Arm's-length, as I believe they call it up there?'

'Dealings? In the City? With Edward Avon? I only met him a few nights ago and bumped into him by accident at breakfast' – followed by the unpleasant afterthought – 'Why? You're not warning me off him, are you?'

Ignoring his question, Celia went on scrutinising him with shrewd eyes:

'Only he's a very good friend of mine, you see, darling, is Mr Edward Avon,' she said with innuendo. 'Like a special friend.'

'Not prying, Celia,' Julian put in hastily, only again to be ignored.

'More special than what you might think. There's not a lot of people know that, apart from my Bernard.' Thoughtful sip of ginny as she continued to scrutinise him. 'Only I wouldn't mind you knowing, you see, what with the impressive City contacts you've got, if I knew I could trust you not to blab. I might even cut you in on something, down the line. Not that you haven't got enough already, from what I hear. Can I, is the point?'

'Trust me?'

'I'm asking.'

'Well, that's something for you to judge, Celia,' Julian said piously, confident by now that nothing was going to stop her.

*

It was a very long story, she assured him: all of ten years now, since her Teddy first breezed through that door there one sunny morning with a carrier bag stuffed with tissue paper, pulled out a Chinese porcelain bowl, put it on the counter and demanded to know what she reckoned it was worth on a good day:

'Am I buying or selling, I say, because I don't know him, do I? He walks in, he says I'm Teddy, like he's my best friend, and I've never seen him in my life. So what you're asking for, I say, is a free valuation, which is not how I make my living, so it's half of one per cent of whatever I say it's worth. Come on, Celia, he says, don't be like that. Just give me a ballpark figure. If I'm buying, I tell him, ten quid, and I'm being generous. Make it ten grand and it's yours, he says. Then he shows me the valuation from Sotheby's. Eight grand. Well, I didn't know who he was, did I? He could have been any joker. Plus he's a bit foreign. Plus I know bugger-all about Ming blue-and-white. Anybody would have guessed that, just looking through the window. Who are you anyway? I say. Avon, he says, first name Edward. Well, I say. Not the Avon that's married to Deborah Garton down at Silverview? The same, he says, but Teddy to you. Because he's like that.'

Julian needed to get his bearings:

'Silverview, Celia?'

Big dark house on the other side of town, darling. Halfway down the hill from the water tower, lovely garden, or was. Used to be called The Maples in the Colonel's day, until Deborah inherited. Now it's Silverview, don't ask Celia why.

And the Colonel was who? Julian asked, trying hard to imagine Edward in this unlikely setting.

Deborah's father, darling. Town benefactor, art collector, founder and patron of the town library, and hands all over you. My Bernard had a contract with him to supply and maintain his gardens. Deborah still has Bernard up there now and then.

And it was the Colonel bequeathed her all his lovely blue-and-white porcelain, Celia went on with a grim sigh. A truly *grande* collection, she insisted, *grande* to rhyme with *horned*.

'So when Teddy walked in on you that day, he was hoping to flog you a bit of family Ming on the side,' Julian suggested, only to see Celia's mouth open and close again in horror.

'Teddy? Bilk his own wife out of her inheritance? He wouldn't ever, darling! He's as straight as a die, is my Teddy, don't ever let anyone tell you different!'

Suitably chastened, Julian waited to be corrected.

No, what Teddy would like to do in his retirement, Celia said, using the funds he'd earned after all those years teaching abroad in places you and me wouldn't be seen dead in – Deborah being away on her quangos and whatever else she was up to – was to raise the quality of the Colonel's grande collection to the absolute tops, partly by trading up, partly by acquisition.

'Plus he'd like his Celia to be his intermediary, scout, purchasing agent and representative on a highly private and confidential basis never to be revealed, with an annual floor commission of two thousand quid cash-in-hand for her trouble, and an agreed percentage of the annual turnover, in cash or kind, with nobody troubling the Inland Revenue, what does she think? Well, what would you think?'

'All this in one short visit to your shop?' Julian exclaimed, privately recalling the eerie speed with which Edward had become prospective co-founder and consultant to the Republic of Literature, all in the space of a cheese omelette.

'Three, darling,' she corrected him. 'One the same afternoon, and then next morning, he's got two grand in tenners in an envelope, he'd got them all ready for the moment I said yes, and there's a piece for me each time he does a deal, him to decide how much – which I can't object to, seeing he'll be doing it all himself anyway behind the scenes.'

And you said?

'I said I'd have to ask my Bernard. Then I said – which I should have said before if I'd known him better – in heaven's name, why come to me? Because you don't sell top-class Chinese blue-and-white porcelain out of a toffee shop, do you? I said. Or buy it, I said. Plus the fact it's all computers and eBay these days, and I haven't even got a computer, let alone know how to work one. We're Luddites, me and Bernard, proud of it, I said. Everybody in the town knows we're Luddites. Didn't bother him a bit. He knew it coming in, he said, he'd got it all worked out in his head. Celia, dear, he says to me, you don't have to lift a finger beyond being who you are. I'll be there for you every inch of the way. I'll buy a computer. I'll instal it and handle it. I'll locate the pieces to buy, and the pieces to trade. I'll study the auction prices. All I ask, he said, is you do the talking, you be my front office under my guidance where needful because I like my life in the shadows, and that'll be my retirement taken care of.'

Celia pursed her lips and took a sip of ginny and a puff of cigarillo.

'And you did all this, just the two of you?' Julian asked bemused. 'For ten years or whatever it was you said. Teddy trades, you take your retainer and your commission.'

*

Julian's bemusement was further compounded by the fact that Celia's mood had blackened dramatically.

For ten long years, ever since day one, everything had gone sweet as sugar. The computer duly arrived and was awarded its own little home – over there, darling, on the bow-fronted escritoire, not six feet from where you're sitting. Edward would drop by whenever he felt like it, not every day by any means, sometimes not every week. He'd sit down in that chair there, with all his catalogues and trade rags, and he'd tap away and they'd have a ginny and Celia would take the calls and front for him.

And every month, rain or shine, there'd be an envelope for her and she wouldn't even count it, which was how much they trusted each other. And if Edward were away on business, which he sometimes was, there'd be the same envelope by registered post, and like as not a billy-doo saying he'd missed her beautiful eyes or something equally daft, because Teddy always knew how to pull out the stops, and he must have been a terror when he was young.

'Away on what sort of business, Celia?'

'International, darling. Education and similar. Edward's an intellectual,' she replied loftily.

Another sigh, a prudish tug at her neckline in case she was giving Julian ideas by mistake, as she approached the moment that ended her ten years in paradise.

It's Sunday night, a week ago. Eleven o'clock, the phone rings. Celia and Bernard have got their feet up, watching telly. Celia picks up the receiver. Her Deborah Avon voice is part Lancashire, part Her Majesty:

'Is this Celia Merridew by enny chance? Yes, Deborah, I say, this is Celia. Well, Ay wish to inform you that Edward and Ay have decided to dispose of our collection of Chaynese blue-and-white porcelain forthwith. Dispose of it, Deborah? You don't mean your grande collection? Yes, Celia, that's exactly what Ay mean. We want it out of the house, preferably by tomorrow latest. All right, Deborah, I say. So where are we supposed to put it? Because you don't shove a grande collection up against any old wall for the night, do you? Well, Celia, she says, seeing as how you've made yourself a small fortune out of Edward over the years, and since Edward assures me you have ample space, how about storing it in your beck area?

'You store it in your back area, I thought – but I didn't say it, did I, because of poor Teddy. Next afternoon, four o'clock by royal appointment, we're up The Maples, all right, Silverview. Bernard's got his tea chests and wood-shavings; I've got my bubble wrap and tissue. Teddy's waiting at the door, white as a sheet, and her ladyship's upstairs in her boudoir with her classical music turned up loud.'

Celia interrupted herself, but not for long:

'All right, I know she's ill. I'm sorry. I'm not saying it's the greatest marriage ever because it's not, but I wouldn't wish what she's got on my worst enemy. The whole house smells of it. You don't even know what you're smelling, except you do.'

Julian acknowledged the sentiment, while Celia consoled herself with a sip of ginny.

'So I say to Teddy, quietly, what's all this about, Teddy? It's not about anything at all, Celia, he says. Me and Deborah, in view of her tragic illness, we've decided to give up acquisition, and that's all there is about it. Well. It's past midnight by the time me and Bernard get it all back here into the shop, and all I'm thinking is, what about the insurance, with all the Romanians and Bulgarians roaming the countryside? Bernard makes himself a pile of blankets on the floor. I stretch out on that Victorian divan there. Midday, Teddy calls me up. He doesn't like telephone as a rule. Our dealers will be arranging transportation directly, Celia. Deborah will be going for a private sale in due course of time, which is her good right. Kindly therefore inform me what I owe you for the removal and insurance. Teddy, I say, I'm not about the money, because I'm not. Just tell me what's going on. Celia, he says, I told you already. We've given up acquisition, and that's all that needs to be said.'

Had she finished? It seemed so, and now she was waiting for him to speak.

'So what does Bernard say?' he asked.

'She needs the money for the doctors. I say bollocks to that. She's got her father's money, her private health, and who knows what else from her quangos. Plus she could buy half of Harley Street with her grande collection and have change left over,' Celia retorted contemptuously, stubbing out the last of her cigarillo. 'So what do you say, clever Mr Julian? Because if you're the brilliant young gun I'm told you are, and seeing as our Teddy is your late father's school friend, and is in total denial regarding his former close friend Celia owing to his wife's unfortunate illness – and me having too much tact to trouble him at such an hour – perhaps some nugget of information will come your way' – very angry now, witness the sudden flush in her face, and the rise in her voice – 'be it from Teddy himself, be it from one of your many City friends and admirers regarding the disposal of a certain unique collection of prime blue-and-white Chinese porcelain. Perhaps one of those Chinese millionaires we read about has snapped it up. Or one of your City syndicates. All I'm saying is' – the crescendo now – 'I've not received one brass farthing on the sale, so if you'd kindly keep an ear out, I'd be very much obliged, young Mr Julian, and I will show my appreciation in a businesslike manner, if you get my meaning. Blue-and-White Celia, they used to call me in the trade. They won't be saying that any more, will they? Not ever. Bugger! That'll be Simon, come to buy my gold.'

A cacophony of Swiss cowbells had announced Simon's

arrival. With improbable agility, Celia sprang to her feet, yanked the folds of her kimono over her hips and straightened the Japanese combs in her hennaed hair.

'Slip out the back way, will you, darling? I don't believe in mixing my flavours,' she said, and set course for the shop.

5

While his children were, or were not, relishing Ellen's fictional image of their father cloistered in some Whitehall dungeon, conferring with the nation's masters of the secret universe, the man himself was installed in the economy carriage of a slow-moving Sunday train that with much clanking and groaning was pulling into the up platform of one of East Anglia's more remote railway stations. To the casual eye, he looked like yesterday's man rather than today's, and that was probably his intention: a business suit, not his newest, black shoes, blue shirt, indeterminate tie. A town worthy, you might have thought; a local council official, grateful for a bit of Sunday overtime.

And, like other people in the carriage, he was reading text messages. All were *en clair*:

Hi Dad! OK borrow Vv w/e Mum away? Jack

Mum: DON'T DIG NEAR SYRIAN BORDER!!! Tell her Dad!!!
Love you, Katie ☺

And from his assistant Antonia at eleven thirty last night: Global research confirms NO historic independent segment recorded, A.

And from his Vice Chief: Stewart for Christ's sake don't frighten the horses. B.

A Royal Air Force truck with white markings on the bonnet stood on the far side of the concourse. A bored Corporal driver sat at the wheel, eyeing Proctor's approach.

'Name?'

'Pearson.'

The Corporal checked his list.

'To see?'

'Todd.'

The Corporal driver reached an arm through the window. Proctor handed him a battered card in a plastic folder. The Corporal driver shook his head, removed the card from its folder, shoved it into a cavity in his dashboard, waited and returned it.

'Know what time you're coming back at all?'

'No.'

Seated at the driver's side, Proctor stared at flat fields rushing by. Suffolk Dog Day was approaching. A regiment of roadside posters told him so, but he couldn't catch the date. After half an hour, a stencilled arrow pointed down a rutted concrete road with wild grass growing in the middle lane. Ahead of them rose a portentous arched gateway like the entrance to a once-great Hollywood studio. A much-repainted Spitfire on stilts flew eternally over it. Proctor got out. Sentries in battle fatigues cradled their automatic rifles like swaddled babies. Above him the flags of Great Britain, the United States and NATO drooped flaccidly in the mid-morning sun.

'Know what time you're coming back?'

'You asked me. No.'

Inside a sandbagged checkpoint mysteriously hung with paper streamers, a woman Flight Sergeant with a clipboard checked his identity against a list.

'And you're a one-time visitor, civil contractor, British access only, Category Three,' she told him. 'Does that accord, Mr Pearson?'

It accorded.

'And you do understand, Mr Pearson, that while on the base, you must at all times be accompanied by an authorised member of base personnel,' she warned him, looking him in the eye the way she'd been taught.

Riding at funereal speed in the back seat of a Jeep over a shimmering sea of fresh-mown lawn, with the Flight Sergeant and a different Corporal driver in the front, Proctor thinks of anything except the delicacy of his mission. He thinks of cricket at his preparatory school, sweet tea and buns in the pavilion. He thinks of Ellen hovering in her apron in the kitchen, waiting to see who wants breakfast. In a week she'll be off on her great archaeology mission. Since when exactly had she so passionately embraced ancient Byzantium? Answer: since the day she started to lay out her wardrobe for the trip on the spare bed in the room across the corridor from their own. He thinks of his son, Jack, and wishes the boy would care a bit more about politics and less about going into the City. He thinks about Katie, his daughter, and her rugger blue. Had she told him about her abortion? And why should she, since he hadn't caused it? And thence yet again to the accusing image of poor Lily trundling her pushchair down the steps in pelting rain.

The deafening bark of jet engines returned him violently to time present. It was followed by the strains of a hunting-horn and the voice of a Texan woman cooing names over a tannoy. Specialist Enrico Gonzalez had won a lottery. Canned applause. The Jeep skirted a military Disneyland of dazzle-painted hangars and black bombers, and descended a grassy knoll towards a huddle of green huts drawn up in a ring and marked with blue flags. The flags acquired roun-dels, the huts a wire perimeter. The Flight Sergeant with her clipboard marched him in quick time past ranks of ceremonial tulips to a bungalow with a veranda. The red-wood floor was so brightly polished that he could see the soles of his shoes as he set them down. On a flimsy door a memorial tablet proclaimed OFFICER I/C UK LIAISON KNOCK AND ENTER. A clean-limbed man of Proctor's age or older sat at his desk, reading a file.

'Mr Pearson for you, Mr Todd,' the Flight Sergeant announced, but Todd must first sign his name before allow-ing himself to be discovered.

'Hullo, Mr Pearson,' he said, rising from his desk and offer-ing Proctor a perfunctory hand. 'We've not met before, have we? Good of you to turn out on a Sunday. I trust we haven't wrecked your weekend for you. Thank you, Flight Sergeant.'

The door closed, the Flight Sergeant's footsteps tinkled down the corridor. Todd remained at the window until she was safely past the tulips.

'Do you mind telling me what the hell you think you're

doing here, Stewart?' he said. 'Smuggling yourself into my base like a stowaway? I live here, for God's sake.'

And receiving no reply except an understanding nod:

'How am I going to explain you if that phone rings and my friend Hank from across the runway says, "Hi, Todd, hear you've got Proctor over there with you. Why don't you bring him over to the mess for a drink?" What do I say then, tell me?'

'I'm as sorry as you are, Todd. I assume Head Office just hoped that on a Sunday they'd all be out playing golf.'

'Even if they are! We have people from the Agency and God knows where walking through the place all the time. All right, not all the time, but enough. You're Proctor the Doctor, for Christ's sake. Head of Domestic Security. Witchfinder-in-Chief. They know you. What happens if one of them clocks you? An enormous and enduring stink, is what, and it'll be all mine. Sit down, have a bloody coffee. Christ Almighty.'

And, having called for 'Two coffees sharpish, please, Ben' into a speaker on his desk, flopped into a chair with his fingertips pressed to his brow in anguish.

If the Service any longer did compassionate postings, which Proctor doubted, then few men were more deserving of its compassion. If it rewarded loyalty, then the fatally handsome Todd, who had served with unswerving loyalty in the worst hotspots the Service had to offer, picking up two gallantry medals and shedding two wives along the way, had in Proctor's view earned his reward in spades.

'And all's well at home, I hope, Todd?' he suggested kindly. 'Everyone reasonably healthy and happy and so on?'

'All very well, and thank you, Stewart, first rate,' Todd replied, immediately rallying. 'Head Office has given me another year, which will see me out, as you may have heard. I've put a sunroom on the lounge, which will add a few quid to the value, should I choose to flog it. Still thinking about that. Situation a bit unclear.'

'How are things with Janice?'

'In touch, thank you, Stewart. And good friends, yes. As you probably know, I'm very much in love with her. She's thinking about coming back. Not absolutely sure she's right on that one, but we may give it a shot. Ellen well too?'

'Great, thanks. Just off to Istanbul. And would surely send her love. And the children?'

'As good as grown up now, aren't they? I do keep their rooms going. Dominic, he's a bit lost. The wandering life didn't help. Some Service kids love it. Others don't. He's clean, he tells me, which isn't quite what they said at the place where they dried him out. Cooking's his latest thing. Always wanted to be a chef. News to me, but there you are. It may be just up his street. As long as he sticks to his guns.'

'And your ravishing daughter? The one you brought to the Christmas party?'

'No worries about Liz whatever, thank God. Her painter chap seems to be making quite a splash in the world of modern art, if you like that kind of thing. Personally I do. But whether he makes the grade commercially, that's another matter. I do slip her whatever's left over after the exes have taken their whack, so let's hope he hits the big time before I'm stony broke,' Todd said, smiling ruefully at the possibility.

'Let's indeed,' Proctor agreed heartily as the coffee finally arrived.

*

Gunning a clapped-out Cherokee down two miles of empty airstrip at what Proctor reckoned would be eighty miles an hour if the speedometer had been working, Todd was for a few glorious seconds the dashing desert irregular he once had been.

'So it's purely and solely a technical error you're here for,' he yelled over the din. 'Am I reading that right?'

'You are,' Proctor shouted back.

'Not human failure. Technical. Correct? Like this little lady.'

'Dead right.'

'It's a blip, according to Head Office. That was Friday at four p.m.'

'Blip's right. No finger-pointing. Technical blip only,' Proctor confirmed.

'Nine p.m. last night, it was a lapse. Which is worse? Blip or lapse?'

'No idea. Their language, not mine.'

'Come this morning, it was a five-star breach. How the hell do you turn a blip into a breach in ten hours cold and call it a technical failure? A breach is human by any normal standards. Right?'

With the handbrake's help, they had drawn to a blessed

halt. Todd turned the key, then waited for the engine to stop. In the tense silence the two men remained seated side by side.

'I mean how the fuck, Stewart, forgive me, can a breach be technical?' Todd protested again. 'I mean a breach is people. It's not fucking fibre optics. It's not tunnels. It's chaps, surely?'

But Proctor was not willing to be so passionately appealed to.

'Todd. My orders are to inspect the plumbing as a matter of urgency, and report back any possible malfunction. Period.'

'You're not even a fucking technician, Stewart, for Christ's sake,' Todd complained, as they lowered themselves to the tarmac. 'You're a bloodhound. That's what I'm on about.'

The above-ground Conference Room was a windowless railway carriage forty feet long with a television screen making up one end. Imitation windows were decorated with wax flowers and painted blue sky. A plywood conference table with computers down its centre and school chairs to either side of it ran the length of the room.

'And this is where your joint team did its hard work, Todd,' Proctor suggested.

'Still does, thanks very much, when need arises, which I'll admit isn't often. Up here as long as the sun's shining, and down to the Hawk Sanctuary in double time if there's an alert.'

'Hawk Sanctuary?'

'Our dedicated nuclear hellhole three hundred feet below ground level. I'm told there used to be a notice on the door, until somebody nicked it: THE UNTHINKABLE IS THOUGHT HERE. Not very funny really, but in deterrence you take your laughs where you can find them. Want the tour?'

'Why not?'

Todd's tour was a potted history composed for his dwindling trickle of visiting dignitaries. In a couple of years' time, by Proctor's guess, a well-informed lady from the National Trust or English Heritage would be delivering the same lecture, heavily redacted, for the edification of tourists.

The facility, Todd recited, dated from the Cold War, as Proctor might not be surprised to hear. It was designed for one purpose only, namely to store nukes, deliver nukes and, if need be, take hits from nukes, while maintaining Command and Control:

'Hence the storage chambers and an absolute bloody maze of tunnels down there in the netherworld. Tunnels to link all the bases in the region, fighter command to bomber command to tactical command to strategic command to God. All mega-secret, also from you and me. The local joke is, the Yanks hollowed out the whole of East Anglia and left us the crust. Originally, the tunnels held pipes for cable. When cable went out of style, fibre came in and that's where we are today. And will remain till death do us part, and long afterwards. So?'

'So,' Proctor agreed.

'And out of the said fibre optic tunnels comes our completely closed circuit. Sealed off, permanently exclusive to us. Not connected to the wider world. No one using it to buy white goods at a steep discount or answer the distressed appeals of Spanish prisoners, no one unwisely looking at dirty pictures. No adolescent script kiddie or enquiring Dutch anarchist will ever hack into it. Physically impossible. So where the fuck Head Office gets its breach from, if it's not a human breach –'

Todd sat down in a school chair and slumped back, staring ironically at the ceiling while he waited for a reply. But Proctor had nothing to offer but a sympathetic smile. He too was wondering how long the charade must last.

*

'So tell me a little about how your team actually worked in practice, Todd,' Proctor suggested earnestly. 'Works still, of course, when called upon.'

At breakneck speed they had returned to Todd's office for a club sandwich and a Diet Coke.

'Same way it always worked, as far as I know,' Todd replied grudgingly.

'Which was how exactly? Is how?'

'Well, if we're talking Nine Eleven or Shock & Awe or whatever, the show ran pretty well round the clock. The base turned itself into a sort of Pentagon think-tank with Brit appendages. Five-star generals flew in and out like yo-yos. Top brass from Langley, NASA, Defence and the White House brigade. You name it. And our own dear team from around the country: Professor this from Chatham House, Doctor that from the Institute of Strategic Studies, couple of cleverdicks from All Souls or wherever. And away they went, thinking the unthinkable round the clock. Strangelove

stuff. Contingency planning for Armageddon. Where to
draw the red lines. Who to nuke when. All a bit above my
pay-grade, thank God. Probably above theirs too.'

'And was there more specific stuff they would handle,
back in those days? Or was it all just playing the world's
game?' Proctor asked.

'Oh, we still have a couple of regional sub-committees,
even today. Post-Soviet Russia gets one to itself. South-
East Asia used to. The Middle East runs and runs. To a
point.'

'To what point?'

'In Bush–Blair days, mega. Then we got an American
President who was a bit calmer, and business went slack.
Stewart.'

'Yes, Todd.'

'Is this about a technological breach, or isn't it? Because
I'm not cleared for a single fucking piece of paper that
goes out of this place. I'm not on the magic circuit and I
don't want to be. Is Head Office looking up its own arse,
or what?'

'I'm thinking it's looking very hard at the magic circuit,
Todd,' said Proctor, deciding that the time was now.

*

They were standing in the hellhole, known to insiders as
the Hawk Sanctuary, and Proctor's ears were still popping
from the descent. The same plywood conference table
and school chairs. The same giant television screen, dor-
mant. The same row of blank computers. The same vile

strip-lighting overhead. The same imitation windows, wax flowers and blue sky. A sense of a ship abandoned, slowly sinking. A stench of decay, age and oil.

'Brits this side, Americans that side,' Todd was intoning. 'Computers are linked to each other in a daisy chain. The daisy chain is complete to itself.'

'Absolutely no external links, then?'

'When there were bases scattered all over East Anglia, yes. As each one closed, the extension was nipped off. You are now standing three hundred feet below the last active US–UK strategic base in the British Isles, Special Ops excluded. To achieve a technological breach, Al Qaeda or the Chinese or whoever else you please would have to dig a bloody great hole in the middle of that runway upstairs, and be gone by morning.'

'And if an alert were sounded tomorrow – say for the former Soviet Union sub-committee – to convene in fast order,' Proctor suggested, aiming as far away from his target as he decently could, 'it would be: get your players on to the base, whisk them down here and pull up the drawbridge. And if Professor somebody from Chatham House has missed his train –'

'Tough titty.'

'And if it's the Middle Eastern sub-committee, which you say is a bit busier, the same applies.'

'Barring only Deborah. Special circumstances.'

'Deborah?'

'Debbie Avon. The Service's star Middle Eastern analyst, for Christ's sake. Or was. You know Debbie. She came to you once, she told me. She asked me whether you were the go-to man if she had a personal security problem to sort out. I said you were.'

'Did I hear was, Todd?'

'She's dying. Didn't Head Office tell you? Jesus Christ. If that's not a technological fault, what the hell is?'

'Dying of what?'

'The big C. She's had it for years. She went into remission, then unremitted again and now it's terminal. Called me up and said goodbye, sorry if she'd been a cow now and then. I said, not now and then – all the time. I was blubbing and she was being Deborah. I just can't believe they didn't tell you.'

Intermission while they agreed that it was high time somebody in Human Resources pulled their socks up.

'Then she told me to have the link disconnected forthwith, because she wouldn't be needing it any more. I mean, Jesus.'

'When was that, actually, Todd?'

'A week ago. Then she rang again to make sure I'd done it. Typical.'

'And you said she was exceptional in some way: barring Deborah, I think you said.'

'Did I? Yes, well, that was a bit of luck. Debbie's got a palatial mansion five miles down the road from here. Used to be her father's when he was in the Service. It turned out that it was on the direct pipeline to a base near Saxmundham that's gone the way of all flesh. Bang in the midst of heavy Middle Eastern stuff. Debbie had had a bad patch and was on chemo, but, being Deborah, she didn't want to let the side down. And the Service didn't want to lose its top analyst. It cost next to nothing to drill down and join her up.'

Todd had a frightful thought:

'But for Christ's sake, Stewart, let's not go thinking that's your technological breach! She's the absolute end of the chain, was, and there's nothing around her for miles.'

To which Proctor replied, take it easy, Todd, we all know what Head Office is like when it gets a bee in its bonnet.

*

Back in Todd's office, while they waited for the Flight Sergeant to arrive with her Jeep, the conversation turned once more to poor Deborah Avon.

'Never been to her place, mind,' Todd mused regretfully. 'Too late now. I'd go like a shot, if she'd let me. The Service was one thing, her private life another. There's a husband somewhere, I heard, not from her. Bit of a drifter, someone said. Bit of teaching, bit of aid work. Abroad a lot. No children mentioned. I asked her once who she had in her life. She as good as told me to mind my bloody business. Have you found it?'

'The breach? I shouldn't think so. Storm in a teacup, by the looks of it. God knows what they're after. If I don't get back to you in a couple of days, assume it's blown over. And make sure you look after that son of yours, Todd,' he added, as the Jeep drew up outside. 'The country needs all the good cooks it can get.'

*

Standing outside the toilet in the jangling space between two elderly carriages, Proctor texts his Vice Chief:

Unrecorded link confirmed. Link discontinued one week ago at Subject's personal request.

He is minded to add: another example of Head Office's failure to join up dots, but as so often restrains himself.

6

Twelve paperback copies of W. G. Sebald's *The Rings of Saturn* arrive by special delivery. Julian takes one for himself and each evening manages a couple of dozen pages, googling great names from world literature before he falls asleep.

He makes a duty trip to London, checks his flat and reminds the estate agents that he has been pressing for a quick sale. They tell him the market is going through the roof, so why not hold off for a couple more months and clean up an extra fifty grand?

For old times' sake he calls on an ex-girlfriend who is about to marry a rich trader. The rich trader is not in evidence, and the time turns out to be not quite as old as he thought. Only by the skin of his teeth does he escape with his honour vaguely intact.

He undertakes a one-day pilgrimage to the nearby town of Aldeburgh, sits at the feet of the proprietors of an independent bookshop of national renown, talks festivals and book clubs, vows to study and learn. He comes away convinced he will never make the grade however many Sebalds he reads; then, with the spring reaching hopefully for an early summer, cheers up. Real people are coming into the shop, and amazingly they're even buying books. But Edward Avon is not among them, and with each day that passes the Republic of Literature becomes a more distant dream.

Is it conceivable that Deborah has died and Julian hasn't heard? The local rag doesn't seem to think so, neither does the local radio, and Celia and Bernard are on holiday in Lanzarote.

'Teddy, he don't come no more, my dear,' Adrianna assures him, when he drops in at the greasy spoon in the course of his morning run. 'Maybe she tell him, Edvard, you good boy, you stay home now.'

And Kiril?

'Kiril don't work NHS no more, my dear. Kiril he gone private.'

A replacement must be found for the departed Bella. A single advertisement elicits a flood of unsuitable applicants. He interviews two a day.

And, come closing time, he walks. Morning jogs are for the body, evening walks for the soul. Ever since he bought the shop he has promised himself that one day soon he will get his boots on and pound the streets of his adopted town. And not just the streets beloved of summer tourists, with their Norman church of brick-and-flint that for a thousand years has served as a watchtower for our loyal citizens and a marker for our gallant mariners out to sea – see last year's guidebook, marked down to £5.96 while we wait interminably for the new one to come in. Not just its pastel-painted Victorian hotels, olde-worlde boarding houses and stately

Edwardian villas that line the seafront either. He means the real streets, the workers' terraces and fishermen's back alleys ten feet wide that run like ruled lines from the tree-lined hilltop to the shingle shore.

Now at last, with the shop's refit complete save for the shelving in the basement, which he has set aside for the day of completion, he feels free to strike out into the urban landscape with all the pent-up zest of a man aching to expand the borders of his new life and rid himself of his old one. No more air-conditioned treadmills, sunlamps and saunas for him, thank you; no more alcoholic revels to celebrate another dicey, socially useless financial coup, and the one-night stands that inevitably follow. London man is dead. Welcome to the small-town bachelor bookseller with a mission.

All right: it's true that now and then, chancing to make eye contact with beautiful strangers, he is assailed by memories of his more shaming excesses, and offers his contrition to the respectable houses with their lace curtains and shimmering television screens. But when he turns another corner or crosses another street, his conscience takes a rest. Yes, yes, I was that man and worse. But I'm a better man now. I have forsaken the glitter of gold for the scent of old paper. I am making a life worth the name, and there's more to come.

Only Matthew, the 22-year-old out-of-work stage designer whom in desperation he has temporarily engaged, dares question his determination. Looking up from the storeroom desktop to discover Julian in full gear – walking boots, waterproofs, oilskin hat – and, outside, the same drenching rain that has been beating down the high street all day long, he lets out a cry of honest dismay:

'You're not going out in this weather, are you, Julian? You'll catch your death.' And, receiving no answer but an employer's forbearing smile: 'I don't want to think what you're punishing yourself for, Julian, I really don't.'

*

No wonder, then, that in the course of these nocturnal meanderings he should find himself, more often than he might care to admit, plodding up the wooded hill on the far side of town and negotiating a puddled lane that runs beside the stone wall of an abandoned schoolhouse, then down an incline to a pair of fine wrought-iron gates grandly titled SILVERVIEW. On a paved forecourt stand three cars in darkness: an old Land Rover, a Volkswagen Beetle and a people carrier marked with the insignia of the local hospital.

Below the house, two tiers of garden descended towards the sea. Was marital harmony restored? Gazing at Silverview, he tried his hardest to believe it was. Adrianna and her Kiril were romancing. Edward was this very minute crouched faithfully at his Deborah's bedside, just as Julian crouched at his mother's in her hellish rest home with the airless stench of stale food and old age, and the singsong rattle of clapped-out trolleys and the chatter of underpaid nurses echoing up and down the corridor.

There was another view of the house, he discovered: a better one if you didn't mind a bit of trespassing, which he didn't. Go down the hill a hundred yards to the new medical centre, cross the car park at the back, ignore the hysterical injunction to proceed no further on pain of death, duck under a wire fence, clamber up a rubble mound beside the transformer station, and there's the same house frowning down on you, with four big French windows on the ground floor, all thickly curtained with only slivers of light to either side; and a fifth window that might belong to a kitchen; and on the first floor, another row of windows, of which only two were lit, one at either end of the house and as far apart from each other as it was possible to get.

And perhaps it was in one of these windows, on one of his forays, that Julian did indeed glimpse the lonely shadow of the white-haired Edward Avon pacing back and forth. Or perhaps by wishing for the man he made him happen, because next evening, after a morning spent extolling the charms of an arts festival to a reluctant town council, who should he find hovering in the shop's doorway just a few minutes after closing time but Edward Avon in his Homburg hat and fawn raincoat, asking to be let in?

'I am not importunate, Julian? You have a moment for me?'

'As many as you like!' Julian cried, with a laugh, wincing as before at the unexpected strength of the handshake.

But he resisted absolutely the impulse to hurry Edward down to the empty basement. There was a certain matter to be got out of the way. For that purpose, the newly opened coffee bar offered a less emotive setting.

*

The Gulliver is Julian's lure for book-reading mums and their offspring. It is stowed away at the top of a magic staircase peopled with elves and pixies in pointed red hats. On its walls, a genial Gulliver dispenses books to little people. Child-height plastic chairs, tables and bookcases adorn its easy-clean floor area. Behind the coffee counter, a Gulliver-themed pink mirror runs the length of the wall.

Julian draws two double espressos from the new machine. Edward takes a hip flask from the side pocket of his raincoat and pours a shot of Scotch into each cup. Does this very aware man sense a certain tension in the air? By now, Julian has had time to examine him under the overhead light. Edward has changed, as might any man whose wife is dying: the gaze is more inward, the jaw is crisper and the more determined for it, the flowing white hair more disciplined. But the infectious smile is as disarming as ever.

'There's one thing we need to sort out, if that's all right by you,' Julian begins, allowing a heavier note to enter his voice by way of warning. 'It concerns your relationship with my late father.'

'But of course! By all means, my dear fellow. You have every right.'

'It's just that I seem to remember you told me that, when you read in a British newspaper about him being disgraced, defrocked and so on, you very generously wrote him a letter offering money, comfort and whatever else he needed.'

'It was the least I could do as his friend,' Edward replies gravely, sipping at his spiked coffee in the pink mirror.

'And all very laudable. Only, when he died, I went through

all his correspondence, you see. Dad was a hamster. He didn't throw a lot away.'

'And you didn't find my letter to him?' – Edward's ever-mobile face registering honest alarm.

'Well, there was just one unexplained bit of mail,' Julian concedes. 'An envelope with a British stamp and a Whitehall postmark. And inside it a handwritten letter – more scrawl, to be honest – on the stationery of the British Embassy in Belgrade. It offered money and help of a sort and it was signed Faustus.'

Edward's face in the mirror registers momentary alarm, then recovers itself in an amused smile, but Julian plunges on.

'So I wrote back, all right? Dear Mr or Ms Faustus, thanks and so on, but I'm sorry to tell you my father's dead. Then about three months later the Embassy returned my letter with a snotty note saying it had no Mr or Ms Faustus on its books and never had done,' he ends, only to find Edward's face smiling at him even more broadly from the mirror.

'I am your Faustus,' he declares. 'When I arrived at our appalling school I was credited by my colleagues, for reasons I can well understand, with an alien air and a brooding disposition. In consequence I was dubbed Faustus. When later I wrote to H. K. in his distress, I hoped that the use of his old friend's nickname might strike a fond chord. Alas, it appears I was mistaken.'

The relief that overcomes Julian at this news is greater than he has allowed himself to imagine; neither is it lost on Edward, as their laughing faces in the mirror meet.

'But what on earth were you doing in Belgrade of all

places?' Julian protests. 'You must have been sitting there in the middle of the Bosnian War.'

Edward is not as quick to answer this question as Julian might expect. His face has fallen into shadow, and he is plucking reminiscently at his lip.

'Indeed, what does one do in a war, my dear fellow?' he asks, as of any reasonable man. 'One does one's best to stop it, of course.'

'Let's have a look downstairs,' Julian suggests.

★

They were standing shoulder to shoulder. Neither man had spoken, each lost to his thoughts. The rising damp had been cured. The basement, according to the architect, was now one big dry-cell battery. The Republic of Literature would not deteriorate.

'Superb,' Edward declared reverently. 'You have repainted the walls, I see.'

'I thought the white was a bit stark. Don't you agree?'

'Is that air-conditioning?'

'Ventilation.'

'The new sockets?' Edward wondered, in a voice that made no attempt to conceal a deeper preoccupation.

'I told them, just spread them around. The more the better.'

'And the smell?'

'Two more days and it'll be gone. And I've got samples of shelving. Take a look at them if you're interested.'

'I am interested. But first I have something to say to you.

As you know but are too courteous to mention, my dear wife, Deborah, is suffering from an incurable illness that must shortly run its course.'

'I did know, Edward. I'm very sorry and if there's anything I can do to help –'

'You have already done so. More than you can imagine. Ever since you conceived the idea of a popular classical library and invited me to assist in its creation, your proposal has been my mainstay.'

I conceived the idea?

From the recesses of his raincoat pocket, Edward had produced a sheaf of foolscap pages folded lengthways and protected against the rain by a plastic envelope.

'You allow?' he enquired.

By the newly fitted ceiling lights Julian examined, with rising enthusiasm if only partial understanding, some six hundred titles with their authors, each one carefully written out in a touchingly foreign hand. Edward meanwhile had tactfully turned his back, and was undertaking a study of the electric sockets.

'You would consider my suggestions a fair basis from which to proceed?'

'More than fair, Edward. Fantastic. Really, thanks. When do we begin?'

'No omissions spring to mind?'

'None I can think of offhand.'

'Some will be hard to acquire. It is unlikely we shall ever be complete for any prolonged period of time. This is of the nature of the project you have engendered. It is a discourse between books, not a museum.'

'It's great.'

'I am relieved. And this hour of day is acceptable? While my wife has her early-evening rest?'

An evening routine was quickly established. No sooner had Matthew wheeled his bicycle into the street with a 'cheery-bye' than Edward slipped through the doorway into the shop. His moods on arrival were unpredictable. Some evenings, he wore an expression so derelict that Julian immediately whisked him upstairs to Gulliver's, where he had taken to keeping a bottle of Scotch in a locked cupboard. Sometimes Edward could manage only a few minutes and was off again; sometimes he stayed a couple of hours.

As his moods fluctuated, so to Julian's ever-attentive ear did his voices, from the sonorous to the skittish to the Received English of the so-called gentlemanly classes. Observing these changes of identity, he couldn't help wondering how much was performance, how much the real man. Where had he been to learn these voices? Who was he imitating when he spoke them? But Julian had no wish to be critical. I'm providing a suffering man with the aid and comfort he offered to my father. And in return – the irrepressible City boy speaking out of him – Edward is providing me with free professional advice and an education. Look no further.

As a side benefit he was hearing for the first time nice things about his father: tales of the young H. K.'s pluck, good heart and popularity as the school's leading activist against the Vietnam War.

'And, best of all, I would say, he never grew up,' Edward

pronounced, over an enhanced espresso. 'H. K. kept the child in himself alive, as we all must.'

'Did you keep yours alive?' Julian asked, a bit too cheekily for his own liking. 'Or is it a case of once a Patrician, always a Patrician?'

Had he gone too far? Edward's quick face had darkened into melancholy – only to be replaced as so often by a radiant smile. Encouraged, Julian pressed his luck:

'From the little I can make out, you seem to have been a lot more grown up than my father ever was. Dad went to Oxford and got Jesus. Where did you go? You were one of life's odd-job men, you said.'

Edward did not at first take kindly to having his words thrown back at him.

'You wish to know my pedigree? Is that what you're asking?' And, before Julian could protest: 'I am no longer of an age to lie to you, Julian. My own dear father was a not-very-talented art dealer of great charm. He escaped from Vienna when it was already too late and, as we dutifully say, never lost his gratitude to England. Neither have I.'

'Edward, I really didn't mean –'

'On my natural father's death – premature, like that of your own dear father – my mother took up with an equally charming violinist, also a man of talent but no money, and off they went to Paris to live in genteel poverty. It had been my father's mistaken wish that I should complete my studies in England. He managed to put aside a little money for that dreadful purpose. Have you enough information about me, or must I continue to explain myself?'

'Absolutely enough. I didn't intend to' – nevertheless something very different was flashing through his head. I'm hearing a tune and it's coming out of my own mouth. I too, now and then, have romanced about my parents.

But mercifully Edward had changed the subject:

'Tell me, Julian. Your fellow Matthew. You have a high regard for him?'

'Very much so. He's waiting for summer, when the theatres open. He hopes they'll need him, and I'm hoping they won't.'

'Can you count on him to stand in for you on the odd occasion?'

'Sure. Now and then. Why?'

Mere curiosity, apparently, for Edward offered no reply. Instead he wished to know, did Julian have a spare computer handy? Julian had several. Might it therefore be sensible for the Republic to have its own email address since Edward was going to conduct searches for scarce or out-of-print works? To both of which requests Julian happily agreed.

'Of course, Edward, no problem. I'll set it up for you.'

And by the next evening Edward had his computer, the Republic had its separate address, and Julian was landed with a daft image of himself as Celia's successor.

But successor to what? From his City days, he is well used to people exploiting him, and exploiting them in return. He is used to people saying they're doing one thing while doing something completely different. If he were to go Celia's route, he might imagine Edward using the computer to flog off his grande collection behind her back. Well, he promised to let her know if he heard anything, so maybe he should sneak downstairs to the basement and take a peek. He does. Precise enquiries of second hand bookshops and publishers. Requests for catalogues of scarce and out-of-print editions. Of priceless Chinese porcelain, zero – either in Sent or Trash. Meanwhile, in ones and twos, the thoughts of great men and women down the ages are starting to trickle in.

'Julian, my dear friend.'

'Edward.'

The topic is Julian's flat in London. Does Julian still use it occasionally? He doesn't, but does Edward want to borrow it? Oh my dear fellow, those days are long over, thank God. But was Julian by any chance thinking of a trip in the next few days?

Julian wasn't. Mind you, he could always find a reason, what with lawyers, accountants and loose ends of business to tie up.

Then perhaps asking Julian to perform a small errand in London might not be too great an imposition?

Quite the reverse, Julian assured him.

So did Julian have any idea of when these loose ends that he had spoken of might next require his presence – given that the matter weighing on Edward's mind was somewhat pressing in nature, not to say urgent?

'If it's urgent and it's weighing on your mind, Edward, I can go up tomorrow,' Julian replied genially.

'I may also assume you are not inexperienced in the field of love?'

'You may, Edward, if you wish,' Julian exclaimed with a puzzled laugh, and a surge of curiosity that he did his best to conceal.

'And if I were to confess to you that for many years I have maintained a relationship with a certain lady without my wife's knowledge? Would that fill you with distaste?'

Was this H. K.'s best pal speaking? – or the late H. K. himself?

'No, Edward, it would not fill me with distaste' – so tell me more.

'And if the errand I am asking were to involve taking a confidential message to such a lady, might I count on your absolute and permanent discretion in all circumstances?'

Edward might indeed. And on that assumption he was already giving Julian his instructions, which were of a precision to take his breath away:

The Everyman Cinema opposite Belsize Park underground station . . . a copy of Sebald's *Rings of Saturn* for purposes of identification . . . two white plastic armchairs on your right hand side . . . alternative seating available in the rear of the lobby . . . if the cinema is closed for any reason, go to the all-day brasserie next door, which is empty at that hour . . . take a window seat and make sure that Sebald is visible.

'So how am I supposed to recognise her?' Julian asked, his curiosity knowing no bounds.

'That will not be necessary, Julian. She will see the Sebald and approach you. You will then hand her the letter in an open manner and make your exit.'

A sense of the absurd came to Julian's rescue:

'What do I call her? Mary?'

'Mary will do very well,' Edward replied solemnly.

*

Did Julian sleep that night? Scarcely. Did he ask himself what in heaven's name he'd let himself in for? Repeatedly. Did he consider calling up Edward and telling him the deal was off? Not once. Or calling up a friend, and asking his or her advice? He had Edward's much-sealed envelope lying on his bedside table, and he'd given his solemn word in every known language.

He rose early, put on his best casual clothes. What does the well-dressed man wear for a blind date with his father's friend's mistress at the Everyman Cinema in Belsize Park? With Edward's envelope in his pocket, and a paperback copy of *The Rings of Saturn* in his briefcase, he fought his way on to the eight-ten commuter train from Ipswich to Liverpool Street, and thence to Belsize Park, where punctually at the appointed hour he took up his position in a white plastic chair in the empty foyer of the Everyman Cinema, with his open Sebald before him.

And this, presumably, was Mary now, pushing open the glass doors and heading purposefully towards him. And the first blazingly obvious thing to be said about her was that this was no casual amour, but an impressively senior woman of style and purpose.

He had risen to his feet and was facing her, his Sebald in his left hand. His right hand was lifted to his chest, halfway to fishing Edward's unaddressed envelope from the inside pocket of his linen jacket. But only halfway, because he needed to wait until she spoke. Eyes mid-brown and carefully shadowed. Silky olive skin. Age inscrutable: anything between forty-five and sixty-five. Make-up barely noticeable, suit businesslike but not entirely conventional. Long skirt, very elegant, but with deep, practical pockets. If she'd walked out of a power conference in the City he wouldn't have been surprised. He's waiting for her to speak. She doesn't.

'I think I may have a letter for you,' he says.

She considers this. She considers him. Unabashed eye contact.

'If you are interested in Sebald and you are from Edward, then you have a letter for me,' she agrees.

Is she smiling? And, if so, is she smiling with him or at him? The accent could be French. She's holding out her hand. Sapphire ring on wedding finger, no nail varnish.

'I am to read this now?'

'Edward didn't specify. Maybe for safety's sake you should.'

'For safety's sake?' – not sure she approves.

'We could go next door for a coffee, if you prefer. Rather than stand here' – extending the conversation any way he can.

The brasserie is empty, as Edward had predicted. Julian selects a booth for four. She asks for iced water, preferably Badoit. He orders a big bottle, two glasses, ice and lemon on the side. Using a knife from the table setting, she slits the envelope open. Plain white A4 paper. Edward's handwriting on both sides. At a glimpse, five pages.

She is holding the letter to one side of her, away from his line of sight. The sleeve has risen on her right arm. Long white puckered scar on the olive skin. Self-inflicted? Not this woman.

She folds the pages together and returns them to their envelope. She twists open the two Gs of her Gucci handbag, slips the letter inside and twists them shut. Her hands the more beautiful for being workmanlike.

'I am ridiculous,' she announces. 'I have no writing paper.'

Julian tries the waitress. She has no writing paper. He remembers seeing a convenience store a few doors down. Will you wait for me? Why does he ask that? What else can she do?

'And an envelope, please,' she says.

'Of course.'

He runs full pelt down the pavement but has to stand in line at the check-out. When he returns, she is sitting exactly where he left her, sipping her iced water and watching the door. One pad of Basildon Bond writing paper, blue. One pack of matching blue envelopes. For you.

'And you brought me Sellotape. Is that to seal the envelope?'

'That was the idea.'

'Should I not trust you?'

'Edward didn't.'

She would like to smile, but she is busy writing behind her cupped hand while Julian ostentatiously doesn't look.

'What is your name, please?'

'Julian.'

'He knows you as this: Julian?' – head down, writing.

'Yes.'

'When will he receive this?'

'Tomorrow evening. When he comes to my bookshop.'

'You have a bookshop?'

'Yes.'

'How is he is in his heart?' – still writing.

Does she mean: how is Edward's spirit considering his wife is dying? Does she know his wife is dying? Does she, as he suspects, mean something altogether different?

'Bearing up pretty well, considering.' Considering what?

'When will you have an opportunity to speak to him alone?'

'Tomorrow.'

'You are not offended?'

'What by? Not at all. Of course not.'

He realises she is referring to the Sellotape. The strong hands measure a length and seal the envelope.

'When you speak to him, please tell him what you have seen. I am well, I am composed, I am at peace. That is how you have seen me, is it not?'

'Yes.'

She gives him the envelope.

'Then please describe me to him as you have seen me. He will wish that.'

She stands up. He walks with her as far as the door. She turns and, for a thank you, places a hand on his upper arm, and lets her cheek graze perfunctorily against his. Body scent, rising from a bare neck. As she steps into the street, he realises that the chauffeur-driven Peugeot in the parking bay is for her. While the driver hurries to open the rear door, the smart City boy writes down the number in his diary, then takes the tube to Liverpool Street.

*

It was eleven o'clock that night before Julian let himself into the shop, and he felt more tired than he'd ever been in his life. So it took him a moment to understand what he was looking at – yet another envelope, this one pasted spectrally to the glazed door, with a yellow sticker from Matthew reading:

MESSAGE FROM A LADY!!

Thinking he had had enough of secret missives for the day, he opened the envelope.

Dear Julian (if I may),

I have heard such nice things about you. How interesting that your father was at school with my husband. And how good of you to provide him with a much-needed occupation. As you may know, I have for the last ten years, thanks to my own father, occupied the non-executive position of Patron of our splendid local library, which was always one of his great loves, and of which I note that you are an ex-officio committee member. Might I therefore, for all these reasons, invite you to a simple supper at our house?

83

I have not been well lately, so you will have to take us as you find us. All evenings are equally good, so come as soon as you can.

Yours sincerely,
Deborah Avon

'What sort of lady?' Julian demanded of Matthew next morning, as soon as the shop opened.

'Tacky brown duffle coat but ever so lovely eyes.'

'Age?'

'Same as yours. Did you watch *Doctor Zhivago* last night?'

'No, I didn't.'

'She had on the same headscarf Lara wears. I mean it looked like the actual one. Gave me quite a shock.'

7

'Stewart, darling! How perfectly splendid! And what a surprise! Oh, you shouldn't have,' cried Joan on the doorstep, accepting his guest offering of a couple of bottles of red Burgundy.

From the map, Proctor had imagined a charming Somerset cottage covered in clematis, but what stared him in the eye as he climbed out of the taxi was the sort of lurid, green-tiled bungalow that the older village residents would have torn their hair about.

'Stewart, old boy! Bloody good to see you. Still in harness, then? Lucky chap!' cried bluff Philip, debonair Englishman on an ash walking stick, hardly a grey hair on his handsome dark head, grinning ruggedly over Joan's shoulder, then hobbling round her for the manly grasp.

But the rugged grin, Proctor noticed, frozen, and the eye above it ominously half closed.

'Yes, afraid so,' Philip volunteered gruffly, reading Proctor's glance. 'Had a bit of a turn, didn't I, darling? Never knock the dear old National Health Service. They've been first rate through and through.'

'And those nurses were all over you, the hussies,' Joan chimed in boisterously. 'Which brought him back to life faster than anything else. Because really you were dead when you got there, weren't you, darling? Even if you wouldn't admit it.'

Shared laughter.

'And then I thought this place would kill him off after Loganberry Cottage, which he adored. It was all I could find for us in a hurry that was on one floor. But he's in his seventh heaven. He's got a beautiful physio lady who comes once a week and he's discovered his suburban self. You'll be needing gnomes in the garden soon, won't you?'

'Painted ones,' Philip said, amid more hoots of laughter.

Was this really the golden couple Proctor remembered from twenty-five years ago? Stroke-smitten Philip bowed over a stick, and Joan a horsy woman in elastic-topped slacks and a t-shirt with a wide-angle print of Old Vienna across her expansive bosom? But Proctor could remember when she was the improbably beautiful Director of Levantine Operations, while husband Philip smoked his pipe and ran the Service's Eastern Europe networks from an outstation next to Lambeth Palace. The best and brightest of the Service's married couples, went the word. And when Philip got the upgraded Belgrade Station at the outbreak of the Bosnian War, and Joan was appointed his number two, you could have heard the applause all the way down to Pay & Allowances in the basement.

In a living–dining room with a picture window looking on to the tiny vegetable garden and beyond it the medieval church where Joan did her twice-monthly stint as flower lady, they relished her bœuf bourguignon and Philip's potatoes and Proctor's Burgundy, and cheerfully discussed the state of Britain – dire – Afghanistan – hopeless, should cut our losses and get out – and the omniscience of their black Labrador bitch whose name, unexplained, was Chapman.

It was not until they had settled over coffee and brandies in the tiny conservatory that, by unspoken consent, they felt free to talk about whatever it was that had brought Stewart to their door. For it was a general truth of Intelligence professionals of a certain age that if sensitive matters are to be discussed at all, then best in a bare room with no party walls and no chandelier.

Joan had donned a pair of heavy-rimmed granny spectacles and enthroned herself on a tall rattan chair that made a halo behind her head. Philip sat knees wide on a carved Indian chest with a lot of cushions on it, and was holding the crook of his walking stick to his chin with both hands. Chapman had stretched herself at his slippered feet. On Joan's orders, Proctor had taken the rocking chair – but mind you don't lean back too far.

'So you're the history-boy these days,' she remarked, picking up on the little that Proctor had told her over the phone.

'Well, indeed,' Proctor agreed heartily, putting a brave face on it. 'I have to admit that when they called me in, I thought they were going to tell me my time was up. Instead of which, they offered me this really rather interesting remittance job.'

'Bloody lucky,' Philip growled.

'Entailing what?' Joan said.

'Being a spare wheel at Training Section, basically,' Proctor confessed. 'Main job: putting together sanitised case histories as teaching tools for new entrants. Under the general heading of "Agent Handling in the Field". Partly to be used as lecture material, and partly for mock exercises.'

'Could have done with some of that ourselves when we joined, couldn't we, darling?' – Philip again. 'No training worth a damn in our day.'

'Two weeks on how to file bumf,' Joan confirmed, her clever, bespectacled eyes still on Proctor. Buying none of it. 'So where do we come in, Stewart?'

Proctor was only too pleased to tell her:

'Well, obviously, whenever we can, we like to include the living witness of the main players. Desk officers, analysts and, crucially, for the warm-body effect, the agent's former handlers.' Philip was busy fondling Chapman's ear, but Joan's steady gaze had not shifted from Proctor's face.

'What an extraordinary expression,' she exclaimed with a sudden bark of laughter. 'The warm-body effect. How very saucy. Did you make it up on the spur of the moment, Stewart? Just for us?'

'Of course he didn't, darling. Don't be bloody silly. We're out of touch. They've got a whole new language. And line managers. And bloody Human Resources instead of a perfectly decent Personnel Department. And focus groups instead of getting on with the job.'

'So, assuming you're both up for it,' Proctor continued, undeterred, 'there's one particular case history we think would repay study, and happily it concerns both of you, so we get two for the price of one, as it were. And, in the hope you are both up for a thorough grilling' – light joke – 'I've brought along the standard letter from Secretariat authorising you to speak exactly as you feel. Go as deep and wide as you like, don't hold back any criticisms you may have of Head Office' – snort from Philip – 'and any necessary redacting will be done our end. And one very important thing from the outset: please don't concern yourselves with what you think we have on file. Agent files, as you two know better than most, are famous for what they don't say. And the old files are even worse than the new ones. Most of what goes on in the field never gets to the paper stage at all, which is probably just as well for all concerned. So the trainers' advice – actually, it's a plea – is assume total ignorance on our part. Tell it to us from new, tell it how it was for you personally, not just for the Service, and let it all hang out. And if you should feel a burning need to slag off Head Office, don't go worrying about your pensions, or any of that nonsense.'

An extended silence, and to Proctor's ear a slightly disconcerting one while Joan studied the letter through a different pair of spectacles from round her neck, then passed it to Philip, who read it with equal care before returning it to Proctor with a dour nod.

'So they've shunted the great Doctor Proctor into Training Section,' Joan mused. 'Holy smoke.'

'Only attached, Joan. I've had a good run.'

'So who's our chief sniffer-dog now that you've been sent off in search of warm bodies? Don't tell me they've left the camp unguarded.'

To which Proctor could only shake his head regretfully, implying that alas he wasn't authorised to provide her with details of the Service's current order of battle, while Joan went on peering relentlessly at him, and Philip massaged Chapman's ear.

'And, just to be on the safe side,' said Proctor, resorting to a more formal tone, 'although the subject of the case history we'd like to hear you on is alive and kicking, we do not propose to alert him in any way to our interest. Put officially, all contact with him is strictly embargoed until you're advised otherwise. Is that fully understood?'

To which Joan let out a long-drawn-out sigh, and said, 'Oh dear. Poor Edward. What have you done now?'

*

Opening their 'little impromptu seminar', as he called it, Proctor reeled off a few subject headings that he had arbitrarily dreamed up on the train journey:

'Broadly, we're looking for social origins and formative influences; then comes recruitment, training and management; then tradecraft and product; and finally resettlement where applicable. Philip, how's about you kick off?'

But Philip wasn't at all sure he wanted to kick off. From the first mention of Edward, his twisted face had set itself in stubborn rejection.

'You're talking about Florian, right? UA in Warsaw. That the chap they want us to talk about?'

Florian was indeed the chap, Proctor confirmed, UA being Service-speak for Unofficial Assistant or Head Agent.

'Well, Florian was a bloody good joe. Wasn't his fault the network came unstuck, whatever they're saying now.'

'And I'm sure that's how we'd like to tell his case history,' Proctor said soothingly. 'Positively and fairly. With your help.'

'And don't get the idea I recruited him. That was Barnie. I was still in London.'

Reverential pause while they recall Barnie, the late great Cold War recruiter, habitué of Chez Les-Lee and of the Paris Left Bank generally, Pied Piper, and ever-faithful father to his joes.

'Mind you, by the time Barnie got his hooks on him, Florian had practically recruited himself,' Philip continued defiantly. 'No great trick on Barnie's part to recruit a fellow who was already mustard to go. Wasn't about money or getting his rocks off. Florian was a cause chap. Show him a cause he believed in, he'd go for it hell-for-leather. It was Ania lit his torch for him. Wasn't Barnie at all. Which didn't stop him claiming the credit. Never did. Take credit for any bloody thing.'

Philip might have gone on in this vein for some time, had not Proctor glanced at Joan for help.

'Darling, you can't just start in the middle of nowhere. Stewart may not even know who Ania is. Or pretend he doesn't. You can't pull her out of a hat like a rabbit, can he, Stewart? You're supposed to be doing social origins and formative influences.'

Called to order by his wife, Philip sat sulking for a while, undecided whether to obey her or go on exactly as before.

'Well, I'll tell you one thing about his social origins,' he broke out. 'Florian had the most fucking awful childhood anyone can imagine. You know about his father, I suppose?'

Again, Proctor had gently to remind Philip that he should suppose nothing of the kind.

'Well, the father was a Pole, wasn't he? And a shit. Far-out Catholic of some sort, blazing Fascist, thought the Nazis were the best thing going. Kissed their arses, helped them with their deportations, fingered Jews in hiding and finished up with a nice desk job, packing them off to the camps in droves. Well' – pause to regroup – 'after the war, they got him, didn't they? Skulking on a farm, pretending to be a yokel. Quick trial, no frills, and they strung him up in the town square. Got a good crowd for it too. His wife was no angel and it's rough justice time, so they looked for her too. Couldn't find her. Why not?'

'You tell me,' said Proctor, with a smile.

'Because, come the reckoning, her bloody husband had smuggled her into Austria, and she's sitting pretty in a convent in Graz under another name having his baby. Seven years after that, she's on the game in Paris with her boy in tow. Florian. Two years on she's married to a British bore from one of the big five banks. British passport for her, British passport for the boy. Not bad going for a Polish tart with a dead Nazi war criminal in her locker.'

'And Florian found all this out when?' Proctor asked, writing studiously in his notebook.

'Aged fourteen. When his mother told him. She was worried sick the Poles were going to pick up the trail and she'd be returned to Warsaw with the boy. Never happened. Her false papers were rock solid. The Poles never made the connection. We checked it out all ways up,' Philip said, as his mouth snapped shut in a grimace.

But he had only paused to reload:

'And that was the only thing Florian ever lied about in his whole life, to my knowledge. Couldn't handle his bloody awful father so he romanced about him. Pitched all sorts of different stories to different women. What the hell was all that bullshit you told Gerda, or whatever her name was, about your father being this heroic sea-captain? I said to him. Was that just to talk her into bed? Didn't admit anything, mind. Not after the training we'd given him. Said it was all about his kind British stepfather. Utter bullshit.'

And as an afterthought:

'And if you want to know where his gut hatred of religion comes from, it starts very understandably with rabid anti-Catholicism and fans out from there. That the sort of stuff you want?'

*

'Formative influences?' Philip repeated, rolling the words contemptuously round his tongue. 'Well, Christ, look at his bloody record. All right, we're pretending he hasn't got one. From the day his mother told him about his natural father, he was a red-toothed anti-Fascist, anti-Imperialist Bolshevik, and a pain in the arse at the English public school they dragged him to. Ringleader of the anti-Vietnam brigade, refused point blank to attend school chapel, card-holding member of the Young Communist League. Needless to say, the Sorbonne took him like a shot, filled his head with more of the same, and six years later, there he was, by his own wish, back in the land of his father. He'd done a year at Zagreb, a year at Havana, a year at Uppsala on the way, and here he was, teaching the Leninist–Marxist interpretation of history at Gdańsk University to a lot of unredeemed Catholic Poles under a Marxist dictatorship that wasn't working. Totally un-believable if you don't know your Middle Europe. Run-of-the-mill if you do,' Philip ended combatively.

'And it was when he got to Poland that he had his great apotheosis, wasn't it, darling?' Joan suggested, gently remov-ing his brandy glass before he could refill it and replacing it with a glass of water.

'Absolutely right, Joan! Those Poles did it for him in spades,' he declared with relish. 'One year in Gdańsk, and the Communist message was the biggest con since the invention of religion. And, better still, he didn't tell a bloody soul till he got back to Paris at Christmas, and whispered it to Ania in bed. Marvellous girl, wasn't she, darling? Ballerina. Polish exile. Gorgeous to look at, all the guts in the world, and adored Florian to bits. Right, darling? Right?'

'You went completely gooey about her,' Joan replied drily. 'Thank God Teddy had got her already.'

'And Ania was indirectly responsible for Florian's recruit-ment, would you say?' Proctor asked, jotting something meaningless in his notebook.

'Look here!'

Ramming both hands on the crook of his walking stick,

Philip had risen to his feet and, placing himself back to the windows, assumed Proctor's role of lecturer:

'What your chaps and chapesses have got to understand is that Agent Florian was an absolute one-off, a gift from Heaven. They will never get a joe who is so committed, with such absolutely kosher credentials. He had a five-star Communist past, all absolutely above board, slice it where you will. He was in place, on target, with fully established cover as a minor university don, and documentation to kill for.'

'And Ania's part in all this, again?' Proctor reminded him.

'Ania's family were key players in the Polish resistance. One brother tortured and shot for his trouble, another rotting in jail. Ania was in Paris when they were arrested and she stayed there. Barnie worked the Polish émigré scene, so he knew Ania. Florian all but fell into his pocket. First-rate agents don't come much easier than that,' Philip said, returning to his Indian chest like a performer who has finished his act.

'And his tradecraft, Philip?' Proctor suggested, ticking off another box. 'Could we pull him out for a seminar from time to time? Somewhere you describe Florian as a deep swimmer. My trainees would be fascinated to know what you meant by that.'

Long rumination, followed by a sudden exhortation:

'Common sense. Whatever you do, don't just go with the flow. Go deep. Smell right. Never go solo if you can be part of the crowd. If you've got a treff in Warsaw and there's a faculty bus going, take it. Lend your typewriter to people. Lend your Lada if you've got one. Let them do you the odd favour in return, but never push your luck. If somebody's visiting their old mum in Poznań, might they be so kind as to drop in this book, this box of chocolates, on a friend? Florian knew it all anyway. We just told him how to use it. Didn't do him any good in the end. Nothing did. Networks have a limited shelf-life. I told him that going in. One day it'll come apart, so be ready. Didn't listen. Wasn't that kind of joe.'

*

It was the moment they had been putting off by mutual agreement. Philip's head had slumped forward and he was glowering at his hands, which were clasped in a rigid monkey-grip on his lap. Joan, more composed, was plucking at her hair and gazing through the windows of the conservatory at the church.

'We overworked him, for Christ's sake,' Philip burst out bitterly. 'Never overwork your joe. Rule one. I told Head Office. Didn't listen to me, thought I'd gone native. You're overreacting, Philip. We have it in hand. Take some leave. Jesus Christ.'

Chastened by his own outburst, Philip bestowed a consoling pat on Chapman, who had raised her head in alarm. Then began again in a calmer voice. Until Florian appeared on the scene, he said, the Warsaw Station had been run off its feet:

'Three days of cat-and-mouse to get a simple letter into the domestic mail system. Every locally employed member of the Embassy staff a plant by definition. Everybody from the Ambassadress's cat upwards followed, watched and bugged round the clock. Then, oh glory, enter out of nowhere this squeaky-clean Head Agent from Gdańsk who can't wait to be put to work.'

Another outburst, as vehement as the first:

'I told Head Office, over and again. You can't expect Florian to fill and empty every bloody dead letter box from Gdańsk to Warsaw. You can't expect him to service every sub-agent and walk-in on our books. The Poles are queuing up to spy for us, I said. We're spoiled for choice. But if you drive him this hard, the whole card house will come down. And it did. Our two best joes arrested on the same night. Another next morning. They're not inter-conscious, but any minute now the needle's going to point at Florian. We've got a decent exfiltration plan in place: clapped-out meat van sitting in a disused garage at the edge of Warsaw with a man-sized cavity. Not original, but we'd test-run it and it worked. I send him a crash message: Florian – get yourself to Warsaw now. No answer. Two days later he shows up and starts bellyaching. Says it's his Poland too, and he'd rather go down with the ship. I told you all along, I said, one day the balloon's going to go up and now it's gone up. So shut up and get into the bloody coffin. Ten hours later he's sitting in a country house in Devon, crying his heart out and saying it was all his stupid fault. Which it never was. His tradecraft was first class, not a stitch out of place. It was our signals. They'd broken them. Made no difference, it was all his fault. That's the sort of chap he was. Took the whole responsibility of life on to his own shoulders. A cause chap. And I'd be very obliged if you'd kindly pass that message to your trainees: if Head Office is working your joes to death, don't say yes, sir, no, sir, three bags full, tell them to go to hell.'

'Joan,' said Proctor. 'Your turn.'

But he was too soon. A marital spat had broken out. Proctor was responsible. He had asked – purely out of curiosity as it might have seemed – at what point the love-affair between Edward and Ania had fizzled out, and was it over by the time Edward returned to England, and Deborah appeared on the scene to debrief him?

For Philip the question was superfluous: the affair had run its course, Edward had been putting himself about, Ania had tired of the separation. Her passion was dance, and there were plenty of other men in the world. Ergo, by the time Head Office launched its routine post-mortem into how the network had unravelled – bloody waste of public money, in Philip's view – Edward was 'alone and palely loitering, and fair game for Deborah or any other girl on the lookout'.

Joan vehemently disagreed:

'Balls, darling. Ania adored Teddy and if he'd whistled she'd have come running to him wherever she was, dance or no dance. Teddy arrived in England in pieces. Was he the poor lost Polish boy who'd sent his friends to the wall, or was he the homecoming British hero that Deborah told him he was? Two weeks, the analysts spent with him, locked up in an exquisite English country house with all mod cons: and Deborah mopping his brow and telling him he's the best UA the Service had ever had. Fair game my Aunt Fanny.'

'And Deborah was pretty much the Service's Queen of

Europe in those days,' Proctor reminded them. 'If Deborah said Florian was a star player, that was pretty much the Service's take on him, I imagine.'

But Joan hadn't done with Deborah yet:

'She got him into bed while he was still sleepwalking, and she broke every rule in the book.'

Joan had a point, for all Philip's harrumphing. Service ethics placed an unbridgeable divide between in-house professionals and field agents. For Deborah and Florian, Head Office had made an exception.

But Philip needed his last word:

'He fell for her, for Christ's sake, Joan! She was his Britannia!' – ignoring Joan's hoot of derision. 'That's what he does. He casts a woman in some image he's got of her, then he falls head over heels for the image. She was British to the core, loyal as they come, good-looking and rich. Edward was bloody lucky.'

If his wife was persuaded by this assessment, the moment of her conversion was invisible to Proctor.

*

Joan's opening words of a new chapter, spoken for a larger audience, had a Wagnerian ring:

'Bosnia! Let's pray there'll never be another, we used to say. Fat lot of good praying did. Six tiny nations squabbling over Big Daddy Tito's Will. All fighting for God, all wanting to be top dog, and nobody to like. Everyone in the right as usual and everyone fighting wars their grandfathers had fought two hundred years ago and lost.'

And horror stories that beggared belief, need she add? Mutilations, crucifixions, impalings, random and wholesale massacres, women and children a speciality. She'd expected it to be awful, but she hadn't expected the Thirty Years War meets the Spanish Inquisition. The deal, as ordained by Head Office, was dead simple:

'Phil would liaise with the countless Intelligence agencies that were falling over each other's feet, including the heads of the six warring secret services of the former Yugoslavia, which would have been enough for any man's plate. He'd also confer with United Nations command and NATO representatives, and brief selected NGOs on the state of combat and zones of extreme danger.

'So, basically, you did overt, didn't you, darling? And jolly well too. The more overt you were, the better for little me, because I was just your silly wife, talking to the gentleman on my right at dinner.'

'Surplus baggage, total parasite, should never have been allowed to Belgrade in the first place,' Philip agreed proudly. 'Fooled all the people all the time. You practically fooled me!' – after which, he let out a hah! of pleasure remembered, and poked delightedly at Chapman with his toe.

And while Philip did overt, Joan's first job as his covert number two was to muster the Station's live sources left over from Tito times – Serbs, Croats, Slovenes, Montenegrins, Macedonians, Bosniaks, many of them still on the payroll, believe it or not – and, in a replay similar to the situation that had faced Philip in Warsaw, her crying need was for an experienced Head Agent to get into the field fast.

No wonder, then, that Florian's name was once more on

the table. Had he not in a previous life taught as a young Docent at Croatia's own Zagreb University?

Might not some of his former students and colleagues be occupying high positions in their respective countries?

Did he not speak immaculate Croatian?

And was he not, as a part-Pole and fellow Slav, more amenable, more sexy, as Joan put it, to the warring parties than any pure-blooded Brit could possibly be? Highlight the Pole in Edward, douse the Brit in him, and once again he was God's gift to an overloaded Station.

But would Florian play? Was his quantum of courage exhausted after the Polish fiasco? Had fatherhood made a different man of him? Above all, would Head Office tolerate the re-employment of a former field agent who was now married to one of the Service's most prized performers? Somewhat surprisingly, in Joan's opinion, Head Office would. Who pushed, who pulled, she never knew, but she reckoned she had a pretty good idea:

'The daughter was still quite young. Edward adored her but he wasn't a natural with bicycles and bears. They were rich. They had nannies. After Poland, the Service had tossed Edward a few jobs: courier runs, temping at overseas stations when someone went on leave, hit-or-miss recruitment ploys. And what was Deborah doing meantime? Busily changing horses. She's a career girl. Boning up on the Middle East, which was her newest best thing, and starring at Anglo-American think-tanks while poor Edward was languishing at home spitting at the ceiling and taking his daughter to the zoo.'

They agreed that Philip should make the approach.

Florian might be out to grass, but Philip had had the running of him in Poland. With full deference to his wife, he briefly took back the story:

'I flew to London and went and saw him. Joan's idea. At his house. Her house, I suppose. Sunny day. Big Edwardian pile in East Anglia. And there he was, sitting in front of the television, watching the war going on. The child too. Not all that surprising, knowing Florian. He knew I was coming, so he'd set the stage. We had a Scotch, I asked him how he was, and he said when do we start? Just like that. No notion of twisting his arm, or talking money or pensions, any of that stuff. It was all about who we'd got for sources, and who could be instantly activated. Ask Joan, I said. Joan's going to be your boss from now on, not me. I'm just another Belgrade suit. He wasn't put out in the least. He liked Joan. He'd met her on his R & Rs, and he trusted her, so not a problem. Rather pleased to have a woman in charge of him for a change. Specially a beautiful one. There you are. She's blushing. What he really wanted to know was: how soon he could get out there and start making a difference? I know what you're going to say, darling: all he wanted to do was get away from Debbie. Not true, you see. He'd got a cause again. All he ever cared about.'

'And the cause was – would you say?' Proctor asked, holding Joan at bay for a moment longer.

'Oh, peace, no question,' Philip replied without hesitation. 'Stop it all now. Stop the Fascists. Bosnia was teeming with them, he knew that. Never underestimate Florian's father. Never underestimate Florian's Communist past. My only wise words of advice to you, weren't they, Joan, when you took him over? A radical's a radical. Doesn't matter whether he's an ex-Communist or an ex anything else. He's the same chap. You don't change your reasoning just because your conclusion's changed. You change the conclusion. Human nature. You might sound a warning word to that effect to your trainees too, Stewart, come to think of it, if they're into recruiting ex-fanatics. Always remember what they were, because it's still in 'em somewhere.'

*

The first question, obviously, Joan said, was Florian's cover. This wasn't Communist Poland. This was disintegrating Yugoslavia, and the whole country was crawling with so many weirdos of one kind or another – arms dealers, evangelists, people-smugglers, drug-smugglers, war tourists and all the world's journalists and spies – that only normal people looked suspicious.

Thickest on the ground were relief agencies of every colour and persuasion under the sun, and the most natural habitat for Florian, Head Office decided, wouldn't be a British or Polish agency but a German one, where he could count on the most sympathy from Croats in particular. Since the Service part-owned it anyway, getting Edward accredited to a German relief agency was no big matter. He would start in Zagreb, where he'd taught.

'But Florian wouldn't sit still anywhere,' Joan asserted grimly. 'If the Service had been paying him mileage, he'd have bankrupted us. He positively threw himself at everyone – his old students and buddies, and all his new best friends, wherever they were. Didn't care who they were as long as he was gleaning from them, the hoarier the better. And, believe me, there were some right charmers out there. Fascist doesn't even cover it. He was a particular hit with the Serbs. He'd sing along with them, swoon over their heroic poetry, and hear all about their divine mission to slaughter every last Muslim man, woman and child in the sacred cause of Serbdom. Then bang in his report by radio, or meet up with me in some benighted mountain village.'

'And with the Bosniaks – the Muslims?' Proctor asked.

Though less perturbable than her husband, Joan hesitated, and pulled the kind of face that augurs bad news:

'Yes, well, the Muslims were always going to be the victims, weren't they? That was in the small print from the start. And Edward, being Edward, loved a victim. So the stage was set,' she confided to the vegetable garden, and plucked at her hair.

'There were one or two early signs, as I seem to recall,' Proctor suggested diffidently, breaking the silence. 'Signs my trainees might do well to look out for when they're fretting about their agents' little ways, as we all do. A couple of examples, Joan?' – pen poised.

'The first sign, if that's what you want to call it, which we duly reported to Head Office immediately it happened, was that Florian hugely resented his Serb material being passed to London and on to the Americans, rather than given straight to the Bosniaks. According to Florian, London wasn't getting his stuff to the Bosniaks fast enough for them to protect themselves from the next onslaught. He even had the nerve to suggest it was deliberate, which was utter balls. And London wasn't going to budge an inch on that, how could they? You can't have field agents passing out their own material to local belligerents. And what about Britain's Special Relationship? What about NATO? Which is what I said to Edward: what are you thinking? This is an alliance we belong to, for better or worse. What I didn't know – what we didn't know – was that he'd fallen madly in love with an entire unaligned family in the hills. Secular, which for Edward is practically mandatory, but deeply rooted in Muslim traditions and working for an Arab NGO. But there's no way to keep tabs on every aspect of an agent's private life, is there?'

'No way on earth,' Philip agreed gruffly, lost to his own thoughts.

'So how could we have known? How could anyone, unless Florian made it his business to tell them? Which is what I said to Head Office. What was I supposed to do, what with the Station in Belgrade and Florian all over the hills?'

'There wasn't a bloody thing more you could have done, darling,' Philip assured her, reaching out to give her hand a squeeze.

*

She only ever knew the village in its after-state, Joan is saying. And she'll trouble Proctor to bear that in mind. When it was just another heap of Bosnian rubble and a lot of gravestones.

But the village was Florian's special place. It was somewhere he'd adopted and could come back to whenever he got a chance. At the time, she knew that much. It wasn't a secret place, it was just a very personal place. On the couple of occasions he'd spoken about it – squatting in the back of an aid truck, most likely, while she debriefed him – it wasn't so much the village that he talked about, more the people in it.

But to be frank she hadn't paid that much attention to the village or anyone else. She was more concerned to make sure Florian was all right, fix their next meeting, get his information out of him and funnel it back to Belgrade.

As Florian described it, it was just like any other Bosniak village stuck in a fold of bare hills a day's drive out of Sarajevo. It had a mosque and two churches – one Catholic, one Orthodox – and sometimes the church bells got mixed up with the muezzin, and nobody cared, which Florian thought was just wonderful.

'You'd never get him admitting that anyone was the better for religion, but at least it wasn't ripping people apart, so hooray. When the village had a knees-up, everyone sang the same songs and got plastered on the same hooch.'

So, yes, she conceded, a dream village, but only in the sense that its inhabitants lived together the way Bosnian communities managed to live for five hundred years before everyone went barking mad.

'What made this particular village such a paradise in Florian's eyes was the marvellous family that he'd taken up with, which hardly registered with me at the time, I have to say. He'd drifted into the place on the off-chance of picking up information about local troop strengths, and suddenly there he was, sitting at a civilised family table, with a beautiful Jordanian couple and their adolescent son, discussing the finer points of the French nineteenth-century novel. I don't mean to sound blasé, but that sort of crazy event was par for the course. Everyone was having at least one life-altering experience a day, and usually five. So, no, I didn't listen as diligently as I probably should have done to Florian drooling on about his dream family. I was far more concerned to hear what he'd got to say about troop movements,' she said.

'And quite right too,' Proctor murmured approvingly while he wrote.

Joan is counting on her fingers. Here's what we found out when it was too late. Our painstaking after-the-event reconstruction carried out at Head Office's behest. Was she going too fast for Stewart?

No, Joan, you're doing fine.

'One Jordanian medical doctor. Name of Faisal. Studied and qualified in France. One Jordanian woman, wife to the above, name of Salma, graduate of the universities of Alexandria and Durham, if you can believe it. One thirteen-year-old boy, name of Aarav, son to both the aforementioned. Aged thirteen studying in Amman but it's school holidays and he wants to be a doctor like his dad. Got that?'

Proctor has got it.

'Faisal and Salma run a medical centre under the auspices of the non-aligned, Saudi-funded NGO. Their medical centre is an abandoned monastery at the edge of the village. The monastery has – or had – one refectory, one paddock, one stream running through it. So a five-star idyll. Wife Salma, organiser extraordinaire, according to Edward, has converted said refectory into a field hospital. Husband Faisal is ably assisted by field medics provided by the same Arab NGO. Every evening lorries appear and disgorge their wounded. The hardest fighting is in Sarajevo, but there is fighting in the mountains too. The village sees itself as a sanctuary on account of its clinic. Mistake.'

*

It is after midnight in relatively quiet Belgrade. Joan and Philip are in bed. Joan has just returned from a field trip. Florian has not been in touch for several days, but that's not significant. His last-known treff was with a Serb Colonel of Artillery. The product was good enough to earn a hero-gram from Head Office. The green phone rings at their bedside: agents only, and only in extremis. Joan, the Station's Head Agent-runner, takes the call:

'I get this husky voice: This is Florian. Florian? I say. Who's Florian? Never heard of you. I mean, the idea that it might be Edward, at that point, never even occurred to me. It didn't sound like Florian. I wasn't even sure he knew his own codename. My first thought was, Florian's been taken hostage and this is his hostage-taker. Then I hear: It's over, Joan, in this absolutely flat, foreign voice. Philip's on the extension by now, aren't you, darling?'

'Keep him talking, only thing to do,' Philip replied. 'He knows Florian. He knows Joan. So the bugger's on to some-thing. I signalled to her, keep him talking' – fingers and thumb wagging – 'keep him talking while I get the operator to trace the call.'

'Which of course was exactly what I was doing already,' Joan said. 'Challenge him, I thought. Who's Joan? I said. What's over? Tell me who you are and I'll tell you whether you've got the right number. Then suddenly he's Edward. And this time I know it's Edward, because he's not being Polish or anything else, it's his proper voice. They've killed them, Joan. They killed Faisal and the boy. And I say, that's awful, Edward, where are you, and why are you using this line? And he says he's in the village. Which village? I ask him. His village. And finally I get its name out of him.'

*

What Joan did next was so extraordinary – and in her bald account of it, so understated – that Proctor needed a moment to recognise the sheer audacity of it. Accompanied by one interpreter, one driver and one Sergeant of Special Forces in plain clothes, she simply headed off into the hills. By next evening they'd found the village, what was left of it. The mosque had been toppled, every house blown to smithereens. In the cemetery, an old mullah was squatting beside a row of fresh graves.

Where are your villagers? Joan asked him.

The Serb Colonel took them. The Serb soldiers made them march across a minefield in single file. The villagers had to tread in each other's footsteps or risk getting their legs blown off.

And the doctor?

Dead. The son also. First the Serb Colonel talked to them,

then he shot them both as a punishment for healing Muslims.

And the wife? Did the Colonel shoot the wife too?

There was a German who spoke Serb, but he arrived too late to save the doctor and his son, the old mullah said. He was a German who came often to the village and stayed at the doctor's house. First the German reasoned with the Colonel in Serb. The Colonel and the German were like old friends. The German was ingenious in discussion. He pretended to the Colonel that he wished the woman for himself. At this the Colonel laughed greatly, grabbed the woman by the arm and gave her to the German like a gift. Then he ordered his men back into their trucks and drove away.

And the German? Joan asked. What became of him?

The German helped the woman bury her dead. Then he took her away in his Jeep.

*

Philip was determined that Proctor should have a wash-and-brush-up before he left, and, while he was about it, come and take a quick look at his den. With Chapman leading the way, they skirted the tiny vegetable patch and entered a gardening hut with a desk, a chair and a computer. On the plank wall hung a group photograph of the Service's cricket team, anno 1979. A string bag of drying garlic hung from a rafter. Clay pots of marrow and courgette stood in lines along the wall.

'The thing is, old boy – between ourselves, don't tell the

trainees or you'll lose your pension – we didn't do much to alter the course of human history, did we?' said Philip. 'As one old spy to another, I reckon I'd have been more use running a boys' club. Don't know what you feel.'

*

Every high street business or shop that target regularly frequents.

Any trader target has befriended or gone out of his way to do favours for. Any favours they've done for target in return.

Any instance where target has borrowed somebody's telephone or computer. Records of all incoming and outgoing traffic.

But Billy, whatever you do, don't for Christ's sake frighten the horses.

8

Julian tried on a tailor-made blue suit, decided it was too City and opted for a checked sports jacket. He ruled the sports jacket too jazzy and replaced it with a dark blue blazer, grey flannels and knitted bird's-eye silk tie from Mr Budd the shirt-maker in Piccadilly Arcade, an indulgence from his profligate past. He tied the tie, untied it, took it off and put it in his blazer pocket. He was tying it again for the umpteenth time while he wrestled with the insoluble questions that had dogged him since his telephone call of forty-eight hours earlier.

'Hullo' – woman's voice. Noisy modern rock music playing in background. Music switched off.

'Hullo. My name's Julian Lawndsley –'

'Great. You're the bookshop. When d'you want to come?'

This can't be Deborah speaking. Is it the *Doctor Zhivago* headscarf?

'Well, if Thursday's okay –'

'Thursday's fine. I'll tell Mum. You all right with fish? Dad loathes it but it's all she can eat. I'm Lily, by the by. The daughter' – dropping her voice to suggest that daughters spell doom.

'Hullo, Lily. I'm all right with anything,' says Julian, reeling from the revelation that, after heaven knew how many hours in Edward's close company, he had no idea till now that Deborah Avon had a daughter, let alone that Edward had. Her voice, he noted, unlike her father's hand-picked tones, was fresh and sassy.

'Seven okay for you?' she was asking. 'Mum does early. An hour plus is about all she can handle.'

'Seven's fine.'

*

And this was not the only mystery in his life. The shop's two laptops had gone missing, one from the stockroom, the other from the basement. The police, when they finally arrived, could make no more of it than Julian could:

'A thorough professional job' was the plain clothes Sergeant's only suggestion: 'We're talking a gang of three minimum. One to create a diversion, two to do the job. Do you recall a lady having a fit of hysterics, or an infant reported missing at all? You don't. While the diversion is occurring, Accomplice A slips into your storeroom and helps himself while Accomplice B nips down the stairs to the basement and does the same. Do you recall any ladies in particularly bulky attire at all?' And, dropping his voice to a murmur: 'You don't think it might be an inside job, I suppose? Your man Matthew over there? He's got no form I'm aware of, but they all have to start somewhere, don't they?'

Perhaps the strangest part of the story was Edward's reaction when he arrived the same evening to be informed by Julian that the computer containing his precious classics library correspondence had gone missing. Nothing in his face altered, nothing in the body. Yet, by the waxy stillness of his gaze, he might as well have been hearing his own death sentence.

'Both,' Julian confirmed. 'And you made no copies, I assume.'

Shake of the head.

'Looks like we've lost the lot, then. Still, we've got your paper list and I've got a spare laptop upstairs that'll do the job. Once we've caught up.'

'Excellent,' said Edward, exercising his usual powers of recovery.

'And I have a letter for you' – handing it to him – 'from Mary.'

'From whom?'

'Mary. The lady in Belsize Park. She wrote back to you. It's here.'

Had he forgotten that Julian had delivered a vital letter for him?

'Ah. Thank you. How kind' – though whether it was Julian who was being kind, or the unnamed lady, wasn't clear.

'There's a message with it. A verbal one that I'm to give you. Are you ready?'

'You spoke to her?'

'Was that a sin?'

'For how long?'

'Eight or nine minutes in all. In the brasserie next door. Most of the time she was writing to you.'

'You spoke on matters of substance?'

'I wouldn't call them that, no. Just about you, really.'

'How was she?'

'That's what she wanted you to know. She's well. She's composed. She's at peace. Her words. She's beautiful too. She didn't say that. I did.'

If only for a fleeting moment, Edward's drawn face lit up with the familiar smile.

'I am most grateful' – grasping Julian's hand in both of his own, crushing it and letting it go. 'Thank you again, many times.'

Good heavens, are those real tears?

'You allow?' – meaning: allow him to read his letter in peace while Julian makes himself scarce.

But Julian wasn't quite ready to do that:

'I'm coming to dinner at your house tomorrow night, in case you didn't know.'

'We shall be honoured.'

'Why didn't you tell me you had a daughter? Have I got such a dreadful reputation? I couldn't believe it. It was –'

It was what? He never knew.

Edward's eyes had closed against the world. He let out a long, slow breath. For the first time since Julian had known him, he was, if only for a few seconds, the man who could take no more. Words finally came to his relief:

'For some years, to my deep regret, our daughter, Lily, has chosen to live her own life in London. We have not always been the closely knit family I would have wished. I failed her. To our great joy, she has returned to us in her mother's hour of need. I may read my letter?'

★

Mr Budd's tie accomplished to his satisfaction, Julian took from his fridge the gift-wrapped bottle of champagne that he had this morning bought from the deli, selected an old raincoat in preference to his City overcoat, locked up the shop and, with feelings of intense curiosity mixed with dire forebodings, set out on the familiar road to Silverview. Reaching the unmade track, he passed a battered white van parked in a lay-by, and a young couple fervently embracing in the front seat. The gates to the house stood wide. The front door opened before he pressed the bell.

'You're Julian, right?'

'And you're Lily.'

She was small and resilient, with dark hair cut like a boy's and a mouth pulled tight on the slant. She wore floppy jeans and a chef's striped apron with red hearts for pockets. Her first look at him was long and frank: his blue blazer, knitted silk tie, jute carrier bag with the Lawndsley Better Books logo stencilled on it. She had her father's deep brown eyes. Pulling the door half shut behind her, she took a step downward to his side. Then, in a quaint gesture of relief, she shoved her hands into the pockets of her apron and rolled her shoulder at him in peer companionship.

'What you got in that bag, then, mate?' she demanded.

'Champagne. Chilled and ready for action.'

'Fab. Mum is officially still in treatment, right? But it could

116

be any day. She knows that, and she doesn't like pity. She speaks what she thinks and she thinks a lot, so anything can happen, okay? Just so's you know what you're letting yourself in for.'

He followed her up the steps and with a sense of trespass entered the cavernous hall of a house that, in the language of estate agents, had long been awaiting modernisation. On the yellowed anaglypta walls of his daughter's home hung the Colonel's cracked oil paintings of ships at sea and the Colonel's antique barometers, lined up like soldiers. The only light source was an iron wheel suspended from the ceiling, surmounted with electric candles dripping yellow plastic. At the far end of the hall, a curved mahogany staircase with white grab handles for the disabled rose into the gloom. Was that Beethoven he heard playing?

'Mum!' Lily yelled up the stairs. 'Your guest's here with a bottle of champers! Get your warpaint on!' – and, without waiting for a reply, she marched Julian through an open doorway into an equally cavernous living room with a marble fireplace filled with dried flowers in a copper urn.

Before the fireplace, two grey sofas drawn up against each other like battle-lines. In a panelled recess, dense rows of leather-bound books. And, at the furthest end of the room, yet another version of the well-known Mr Edward Avon of Silverview, waiting to be discovered in faded maroon smoking jacket and matching evening slippers with gold braid. His white hair was neatly combed, and flicked up in little horns behind the ears.

'Julian, my dear fellow! How perfectly delightful!' – stretching out a hospitable hand – 'And you and Lily have introduced yourselves, I see. Excellent! But what is that you're carrying, my goodness? Did I hear champagne? Lily darling. Is your mother launched on her great descent?'

'Couple of minutes. I'll be sticking this into the fridge and getting supper out. When I yell, mind you come running. Right, Tedsky?'

'Perfect, darling. Of course.'

Edward and Julian facing each other. On a coffee table between them, a silver tray with a decanter and glasses. And, in Edward's eyes, something that Julian hadn't seen there before: it almost looked like fear.

'May I tempt you to a sherry, Julian? Or something a little stronger? Obviously, nobody in this house knows of your trip to London.'

'I'm aware of that.'

'It is known that we are creating a classical library section for your excellent shop. I suggest that news of the stolen computers might cause needless distress and is best avoided. Deborah can be oversensitive to certain matters. All other topics are of course wide open to discussion. At this hour of the day, she is at her most alert.'

The Beethoven from upstairs had stopped, leaving only the creaks and whispers of an echoing house. Edward filled two sherry glasses, handed one to Julian, raised the other to his lips and tipped it in a silent toast. Julian tipped his. As if on a nod from the prompter in the wings, Edward resumed their conversation at a louder level:

'Deborah has really been looking forward to this, Julian. Her father's long association with the town's public library is something she greatly treasures. The family trust remains a substantial donor.'

'Wonderful,' Julian said, loudly in return. 'That's really' – he was going to add 'thrilling' but, hearing clanking sounds from the kitchen, elected to ask about Lily instead.

'What she does – for a living, you mean?' Edward mused, as if the question were new to him. 'For the moment, Lily cooks. And cherishes her dear mother, obviously. But for a living' – why was it all so difficult? – 'her forte is art, I would say. Not quite the fine art one might wish for her as a father, but art of a sort is her first love. Yes.'

'Graphic art – commercial art?'

'Precisely. In that category. You are correct.'

They are rescued by the melodious voice of a Barbadian man coming down the stairs:

'Steady as she go, my darlin' . . . one step at a time, now . . . fine and dandy . . . You take it easy, easy now, my darlin' . . . you doin' lovely, just lovely now, that's right' – and to each exhortation, a shuffle of footsteps.

A stately couple is descending the great staircase arm in arm as if it's their golden day: the groom young, black and singularly handsome in dreadlocks, and his lips barely moving as he intones his vows; the bride slender and all in midnight with a belt in papery gold, and silver-grey hair making wings either side of her childlike face, one hand for the banister, the toe of one golden sandal testing blindly for the next stair.

'Is that you, Master Julian?' she enquires sternly.

'It is indeed, Deborah. Good evening, and thanks very much for inviting me.'

'Have they given you something to drink? The service round here is not always what it should be.'

'He brought us champagne, darling,' Edward calls up to her.

'And you found time for us,' Deborah goes on, ignoring this. 'What with all the headaches you've had to endure at the shop. Our local builders are the absolute end, I'm told. Don't you agree, Milton?'

'Sure are,' the bridegroom agrees.

Edward is nudging Julian forward. 'I think best we go on through, is that right for you, Milton?' he enquires up the stairs. 'Chair at the head of the table, nearest the door?'

'Sounds good to me, Ted.'

Edward again, his paternal voice:

'Lily darling, could you turn your kitchen music down before you drive your mother back upstairs again, please?'

'Oops – done. Sorry, Mum.' Music stops.

They enter another desolate room. On a distant wall hangs a bank of conspicuously empty brown wood shelves. Did they once contain a certain grande collection? The dining table is set at one end: damask napkins, silver candelabras, coasters, pheasants, peppermills. At its head, Deborah's high-backed throne, bolstered with hospital pillows.

'Need any help in there, Lily dear? Or will I only be getting in the way as usual?' Edward enquires of an open serving hatch, and for answer gets a crash of plates, the thump of an oven door and a muttered but audible fuck.

'Can I help?' Julian suggests, but Edward is busying himself with the champagne and Lily has more pots and pans to throw around.

Deborah and Milton are performing their private ballet,

Milton holding her by the wrists, leaning back. Gracefully, Deborah allows herself to be lowered into the pillows.

'Nine thirty okay for your rest-time, my lady?' Milton asks.

'One gets so tired of resting, don't you agree, Julian?' Deborah complains. 'Do please sit down. Let others moil, that we may sit.'

Is that a quotation? Perhaps they talk in quotations all the time. He sits. Already he is feeling a surge of affection for Deborah. Or admiration. Or love. She's his mother and she's about to die, and she's being deceived by her husband. She's beautiful and senior and brave as hell and if you don't love her now you'll be too late. Edward is making a business of putting out glasses of champagne on the silver coasters in front of them. Deborah appears not to notice.

'Nine thirty okay by you, Ted?' Milton asks Edward, over Deborah's head.

'Fine by me, Milton,' says Edward, placing a glass in the hatch for Lily.

Exit Milton right.

'We have a lover,' Deborah confides to Julian, once the door is safely closed. 'Secreted somewhere in the town, where we may not know. Nor may we ask whether it's a boy lover or a girl lover. Lily tells me it's impolite.'

'Which it bloody well is,' Lily rejoins through the serving hatch. 'Cheers, Mum.'

'And cheers to you, darling. And to you, Julian.'

Not to Edward?

'Are you fully settled here, Julian, or do you keep one wistful foot in London, just in case?' Deborah enquires.

'Not a wistful foot, really, Deborah. I've no great longing to return. I've still got my flat, but I'm trying to sell it.'

'I'm sure you'll have no difficulty. The property market is soaring, one reads.'

Is this what we do when we're dying? Read about houses we're never going to live in?

'But you still go up now and then?'

'Occasionally' – just never to Belsize Park.

'Only when you have to? Or when you get bored with us?'

'When I have to, and I certainly don't get bored with you, Deborah,' he comes back gamely, making sure not to catch Edward's eye.

He is thinking about Mary. Ever since he set eyes on Deborah, he has been matching and separating Edward's two women. The contest is unfair. Where Mary exuded warmth, Deborah exudes only reserve.

Lily has emerged from the kitchen, first to minister to her mother's hair, which has suffered a perceived derangement on the descent, then to kiss her on the forehead, then to take another gulp of champagne, then to fetch toast and small plates from the serving hatch, and finally to seat herself at Julian's right side, while Edward fusses with dishes and bottles at the sideboard.

'Horseradish for anyone who wants it,' Lily announces. 'Sainsbury's best. All right, dude?' – to Julian, accompanied by a jab of her elbow in his ribs.

'Brilliant. All right your end?'

'Spiffing, old man,' she reports in her best Eton boating-song English.

'And smoked eel, darling,' her mother exclaims in delight, as if the plate hasn't been lying in front of her ever since she sat down. 'My absolute favourite. How clever you are. And with Julian's champagne to wash it down. We really are spoiled. Julian.'

'Deborah?'

'Your beautiful new shop. Will it prosper? I don't mean financially. That's neither here nor there. You're vastly rich, I'm told. But prosper as a quality bookshop in the community? As a cultural sister-ship to our excellent library? Here in our poor little town with all its weekenders and in-comers?'

He is all set to answer affirmatively, but the sting is yet to come:

'I mean, can you really lay your hand over your heart and tell me that a classics library is an appropriate lure for what we must call ordinary folk?'

'He'll make it work, Mum, believe me. He's the boy to watch, right, Jules? I've seen his emporium. It's a literary Fortnum's. Never mind us ordinary folk. The yups will fall for it in droves.'

Her champagne exhausted, Lily takes a swig of white wine.

'But really and truly, Julian, in this day and age?' Deborah insists. 'I mean, are you absolutely sure Edward isn't rushing you into something that is totally uncommercial? He's terribly manipulative when he wants to be, specially where sons of old school friends are concerned.'

'Are you manipulating me?' Julian calls out cheerfully to Edward, who so far has been too busy topping up glasses to take part in any conversation going on within six feet of him.

'Absolutely I am, Julian!' he declares too brightly. 'I'm surprised you haven't noticed already. Keeping your shop open after hours. Obliging you to take in a stray dog like myself every evening. I would say that was manipulation of a high order, would you not, Lily?'

'Well, watch out, Julian, is all I can say,' Deborah warns him coolly. 'Or you will wake up one morning and discover you're bankrupt because he's making you buy all the wrong books. Are you a Christian, Julian?'

His answer was made the more difficult by the discovery that Lily had grasped his hand under the table – not, so far as he could judge, in a flirtatious gesture, but more in the way that she might grab a hand in the middle of a gruesome movie she couldn't bear.

'I don't think so,' he replies judiciously, giving her hand an encouraging squeeze, then gently releasing it. 'Not on present count, no.'

'You have an aversion to organised religion, no doubt, just as I do. Nevertheless, I have spent my life adhering to the superstitions of my tribe, and I intend to be buried according to its rituals. Are you tribal, Julian?'

'Tell me which tribe I belong to, Deborah, and I'll try to be,' he replies, surprised to discover that the hand had returned.

'Christianity for me is not so much about religion as about values we hold dear. And the sacrifices we make to preserve them. Have you by any chance noticed my father's medals in the town library?'

'I'm afraid not.'

'They're ace,' Lily advises. 'Top of the range.'

'We endowed it, you know. Darling, are you sure you should drink so much?'

'I need to build up my strength, Mum,' she says, her hand now nestling in Julian's palm like an old friend.

'In the hall as you enter. On the west wall. They are quite modestly displayed, in a small boxed frame with a brass plate on it. My father landed with the first wave at Normandy and won himself a bar to his Military Cross. You will see it on the ribbon. A bar is a quite modest adornment, but it speaks for a great deal.'

'I'm sure it does.'

'You've got a bar, haven't you, Jules? A coffee bar. Upstairs. Matthew told me.'

'And the Colonel's father died at Gallipoli. Did Edward tell you that?'

'I don't believe he did.'

'No. He wouldn't have done.'

'Eel slipping down grateful, Tedsky?' Lily demands across the table, without at all relinquishing Julian's hand.

'A treat, darling. Just about to get stuck into it,' replies Edward, who loathes fish.

Julian, whose whole life, he has by now decided, has been an extended master class in conciliation, again steps into the gap:

'I'm seriously hoping to stir the town into reviving its arts festival, Deborah. I don't know if anyone's told you that?'

'No. They haven't.'

'Jules is telling you now, Mum,' says Lily. 'So listen up.'

'It's a bit of an uphill struggle at the moment, I'm afraid,' he goes on. 'The powers-that-be don't seem very motivated. I wondered whether you happened to have any wise thoughts on the subject that I could pass on?'

Has she? Hasn't she?

Hand withdrawn while Lily stacks dirty eel plates for Edward to take to the serving hatch and Deborah ponders the question. Her half-glass of champagne has brought hot points of colour to her cheeks. Her large pale eyes are blazing white.

'My husband, who is of a liberal disposition, he tells me, harbours the refreshing notion that Britain requires a new élite,' she proclaims loudly. 'Perhaps you should make that your guiding theme.'

'Of the festival?'

'No. Not the festival. Of your classics department. Out with the old guard, and in with we-know-not-what. Alternatively, of course, one could propose a new electorate. But that would be baying for the moon. Well, wouldn't it?'

General confusion. What does she mean? Edward, having appointed himself kitchen boy, is serving out fish crumble. Lily has returned to the table and put her chin in her spare hand while she thinks distant thoughts. Brave Julian, single-handed as before:

'I'm surprised to hear you describe Edward as liberal, Deborah' – as if Edward is in another county – 'I'd rather cast him as a conservative sort of chap. Maybe it was the Homburg hat that fooled me,' he says for laughs, and wins himself a grateful snort of laughter from Lily, but from Deborah only a glower.

'Then perhaps you should know, Julian, why we were compelled to change the name of my father's house to Silverview,' she suggests, having swallowed the last of her champagne in a single angry draught.

'Oh, Mum!'

'Or has Edward already provided you with a dubious explanation of his own?'

'Neither dubious nor the other kind,' Julian assures her.

'Oh, fuck, Mum. Please.'

'You have heard of Friedrich Nietzsche, I assume, Julian? Hitler's chosen philosopher? Edward tells me that you are a late developer in certain areas of culture.'

'Honestly, Mum,' Lily pleads, and this time jumps up, runs to her mother, cuddles her and strokes her hair.

'Quite soon after my husband Edward and I were married, he came – unilaterally, I may say – to the conclusion that Friedrich Nietzsche had been greatly maligned by history.'

Edward jerks to life at last:

'It wasn't unilateral at all, Deborah,' he declares, uncharacteristically colouring. 'The Nietzsche myth that we were made to swallow for decades was got up by his repellent sister and her equally appalling husband. The two of them spun the poor man into something he'd never been – mostly long after he was dead, I would say. We cannot allow the monsters of world history to appropriate formidable, questing intellects to their disgusting causes.'

'Yes, well, I hope nobody does that to me,' says Deborah, while Lily continues to stroke her head. 'Even if Nietzsche was our most fearless advocate of individual freedom, then what? Individual freedom to me always came with built-in obligations. Whereas for Nietzsche and Edward there are none. It's "Do what you think", not "Think what you do", for Nietzsche and for Edward. A most dangerous dictum, would you not say, Julian?'

'I'd have to think about it.'

'Mum, for Christ's sake.'

'Please do. Edward was so seized by the idea that all one could do was agree with him. Nietzsche's house in Weimar was called Silberblick, so it had to be Silverview for us. And we went along with it, didn't we, darling, all those years ago?' – to Lily, who by now is desperately covering her mother's head in weightless kisses.

But Deborah is not to be quieted:

'Now about yourself, Julian. I insist on being curious.'

'About me, Deborah' – somehow keeping up a playful tone, as Lily once more settles beside him.

'Yes, you. Who are you? You're a blessing, obviously. A mitzvah, as the Jews have it. That goes without saying. But may one ask why you gave up the City in such a hurry? From the little that reaches me, you were seized by some sort of anti-capitalist fervour. Only after you'd made your fortune, but we must set that aside. Are my sources correctly informed?'

'Actually, Deborah, it was more like metal fatigue. Brought on by handling too much of other people's money.'

'I'll drink to that!' Edward broke out, grabbing his glass and raising it. 'Metal fatigue. Starts in the fingers, works its way up to the brain. Well done, Julian. Full marks.'

Another silence threatens.

'So, Deborah. Your turn, if I may make so bold,' Julian strikes up, with the last of his diplomacy. 'I know Edward is a considerable linguist. And you're a distinguished academic in harness to the government, I believe. May I ask what it is you actually do?'

It is Lily who leaps in, neatly rerouting the question:

'Tedsky is a fantastic linguist: Polish, Czech, Serbo-Croat, the whole bag, right, Tedsky? His English isn't bad either. Go on, Dad. Sock it to him. The whole shopping list.'

Edward affects to demur, then shares in the diversion:

'Oh, I'm a parrot, darling. What's the good of a few languages if one's got nothing to say in them? German, you forgot. A bit of Hungarian. French, obviously.'

But it's Deborah's incisive voice, when it finally returns, that seals the moment:

'And I am by profession an Arabist,' she announces.

*

Somehow it's coffee time and, by Julian's furtively consulted wristwatch, twenty past nine, or ten to Deborah's appointed exit. Lily has disappeared. From upstairs, a woman's voice is singing an Irish ballad. Edward sits silent, toying with his wine. Deborah sits upright in her pillows with her eyes closed, like a beautiful horsewoman asleep in the saddle.

'Julian.'

'Still here, Deborah.'

'All through the war, my father's brother Andrew worked not very far from here as a scientist, a very gifted one. Did Edward tell you that?'

'I don't think so, Deborah. Did you, Edward?'

'I may have omitted to mention it.'

'In great secrecy. Which he observed until he died, largely of exhaustion. They were loyal men in those days. You're not a pacifist, I hope?'

'I don't think so.'

'Well, don't be. Here's Milton. On time as usual. I mustn't ask him what he's been doing, it would be impolite. Very good that you came, Julian. I shall remain sitting here. My ascent of the north wall of the staircase tends to be less elegant.'

And with that, Julian found himself dismissed.

Edward was waiting in the hall. The front door stood open.

'I hope that wasn't too painful,' he said brightly, holding out his hand for the hearty shake.

'It was great.'

'And Lily sends her regrets. A bit of family business to attend to.'

'Of course. Please thank her for me.'

He stepped into the night air and with the last of his good manners walked as slowly as he could until he reached the end of the track. About to break into a cathartic jog, he was met by the glare of a hand torch, and behind it Lily Avon in her *Doctor Zhivago* headscarf.

*

At first they walked at a distance from each other, each to his own zone, like stunned people walking away from a car smash. Then she took his arm. The night was grey and damp and very still. The battered van was parked in the lay-by, but its lovers had retreated to the back or gone their separate ways. The poor end of the high street was a sodium-lit orange avenue of charity shops. The rich end was shining white, and Lawndsley's Better Books was its latest pride. Without a word spoken between them, she followed him up the side stairs to his flat. The living room was as sparse as the monk in him had intended it to be: a two-piece sofa, an armchair, a desk, a reading lamp. The bay window looked out to sea, except tonight there was no sea, just dull cloud and tears of rain. She chose the armchair and threw herself into it, letting her arms dangle, like a boxer between rounds.

'I'm not pissed, right?'

'Right.'

'And I'm not going to sleep with you,' she told him.

'Right.'

'Got any water on you?'

He poured two glasses of sparkling water from the fridge and handed her one.

'My dad thinks you're the kipper's knickers.'

'He was pals with my father at school.'

'He talks to you a lot, doesn't he?'

'Does he? I'm not sure. What about?'

'I don't know. His women maybe. What he feels. Who he is. The stuff people talk about when they're being normal.'

'I think he's just sorry he didn't see more of you when you were growing up,' Julian replied cautiously.

'Yeah, well, it's a bit fucking late for that now, isn't it?' – examining her cellphone. 'You were great by the way. Polite.

Slimy. Charmed Mum's pants off. Not a lot of people do that. How do I get a signal in this place?'

'Try the window.'

The *Doctor Zhivago* headscarf had fallen round her neck. Silhouetted against the window, leaning back as she texted, she looked taller, stronger, more feminine. Already her cellphone was peeping a reply.

'Bingo,' she reported, with a sudden luminous smile that was a carbon copy of her father's. 'Mum is great and listening to the World Service in her sleep. And Sam's kipping solid.'

'Sam being?'

'My little 'un. He's got a snuffle and it pisses him off.'

Sam whose mother sings him Irish ballads at bed-time. Sam, the unmentioned grandchild to Edward. Sam, the son of Edward's unmentioned daughter, Lily. Doors opening and closing.

'He's black,' Lily said, holding up her cellphone for Julian to admire a snap of a laughing boy with his arm round the neck of a greyhound. 'Mixed race, if you like, but in a family like ours it's the same. Mum can handle any colour except black, unless they're carers. First time she saw him she called him her little black Sambo and Dad went ballistic. So did I.'

'But you see your Dad in London now and then?'

Why the but?

'Sure.'

'Often?'

'Sometimes.'

'What do you do? Take Sam to the zoo together?'

'That sort of stuff.'

'Theatre?'

'Sometimes. Long lunches at Wiltons sometimes, the two of us. He loves us to bits, right?'

And a 'keep out' warning to strangers.

*

With hindsight, Julian remembered best the quiet that came over them, the peace after a battle they'd fought side by side, the misplaced concerns he'd had about who he'd let into his life. He remembered how their small talk did duty for all the talk that was too big to handle. And how, when Lily spoke about her parents, she managed to skirt round the edge of them as if their real centre were out of bounds. And how, like her father, she tested him out as someone she might one day confide in; just not yet.

No, Sam's father wasn't in the picture. A beautiful mistake for both of them with a great consequence. Line drawn under it all. He visits regularly, but he had a new life now and so did she.

Yes, she was the graphic artist Edward had made her out to be. She'd done half the course and chucked in the other half when Sam came along. The course was crap anyway.

She'd written and illustrated a couple of children's books but hadn't found a publisher. She was writing another.

She and Sam shared a tiny flat in Bloomsbury courtesy of her parents, and she paid the bills with 'whatever design junk comes my way'. Silverview gave her the creeps.

Education – what fucking education? Boarding schools from the day she was born.

Men? Give me a break, Jules. Me and Sam are better off on our own. How about you, anyway?

Julian says resting too.

Arm in arm they walked back through the silent streets, but only as far as the beginning of the lane. Did Lily really believe Edward hadn't spotted her slipping out of the back door, Julian wondered. Edward was the most watchful man he'd ever met. If she'd been a cat, he'd have spotted her.

The battered white van had gone. Ahead of them rose the hulk of Silverview, black against the early-dawn sky. A yellow glow hung over the front porch. A couple of upstairs windows were still lit. Stepping away from him, Lily braced her shoulders, took a deep breath.

'Maybe we'll come and buy a book off you,' she said, and strode off without looking back.

9

'From ten thirty we have no dance but we have consult-
ation, Mr Pearson, until two o'clock,' she had informed
him severely over the telephone in her Polish–French
accents. 'If I am delayed, kindly take a seat in the waiting
area on the first floor and suppose yourself to be a parent
or guardian who wishes to consult me.'

It was ten fifteen. Quarter of an hour to go. Proctor
was sitting in a rundown Greek taverna in Battersea,
trying to pull himself together with the help of a second
thick black coffee, medium sweet. Across the rainswept
street from him rose the redbrick School of Dance
and Ballet. In its arched upper windows, shadows of
young dancers posed and gesticulated behind the drawn
blinds.

He had spent most of the night wading through unpro-
cessed intercept material in order to be up to speed for a
breakfast meeting with Battenby, the Vice Chief, and his
two heads of Legal Department. At the last minute, the
meeting had been put back till this evening. After three
hours' sleep, he was standing under the shower in Dolphin

Square when Ellen called to tell him the dig had made a dramatic find, and it would be unfair on the others if she didn't stay on for a few more days yet, adding by way of a patent diversion that she'd have to talk seriously to the travel agency about her return ticket.

'So you're staying on so as not to be unfair to the others,' he said acidly. 'What exactly have you dug up?'

'Wonderful things, Stewart. You wouldn't understand at all,' Ellen replied with a lofty insouciance that added to his irritation. 'A complete Roman villa they're unearthing, they've been looking for it for years and now they've found it, imagine. With all its kitchens intact and heaven knows what else. Charcoal in the ovens even. They're having a big party to celebrate. Fireworks and speeches, I don't know what.'

Too much information. One lie after another in case the last one didn't work.

'And they found all these wonders where?' he persisted in the same flat voice.

'Out on the dig. At the site, for God's sake. On a beautiful hillside. I'm standing there now. Where else d'you think you find a Roman villa like that?'

'I am asking you where the site is geographically.'

'Are you interrogating me, or what, Stewart?'

'It simply occurred to me that it might be in the garden of that nice hotel you're staying at, that's all,' he replied, and, unable to listen to her torrent of protestations, rang off.

*

Chin in hand, and a third Greek coffee at his elbow, Proctor reread the selected passages of ancient files that his assistant Antonia had transferred to his smart phone:

It is the year 1973. Special Branch has fallen in love:

Subject lives for her dance only. Subject is endowed with all natural graces. Subject, being wholly absorbed in her art, is of no known political or religious affiliation. Subject is regarded by her tutors as a model student capable of ascending to the dizziest heights of her profession.

It is four decades later. Special Branch is no longer in love:

Subject has for two decades been cohabiting with serial peace activist, pro-Palestinian protester and human rights campaigner Felix BANKSTEAD (PF attached). While not regarded as being in the same league as her common-law spouse, subject has come to notice on frequent occasions marching at BANKSTEAD's side, e.g., during the run-up to the Iraq War when, having achieved the requisite number of appearances at listed demonstrations, she was duly upgraded to AMBER.

The shadows in the upper windows across the road vanished. Traffic was at a standstill in the sudden downpour. From an arched doorway, a multi-ethnic group of teenagers emerged and scattered for the bus stops. Proctor paid for his coffee, pulled his raincoat over his head and scurried between grid-locked cars to the opposite pavement.

Not sure whether to press the bell or walk in, he did both, and found himself in an empty brick hall hung with paper sculptures and notices of dance events. A staircase lined with ballet posters led to a minstrels' gallery. A door marked PRINCIPAL was half open. He tapped, pushed, poked his head round. A tall, elegant woman of unguessable age stood erect at a music stand, critically observing his advance. She wore black trousers and a leotard top.

'Mr Pearson?'

'That's right. And you're Ania.'

'And you are a government employee. And you wish to ask me certain questions. Yes?'

'Absolutely right. Very good of you to see me.'

'You are police?'

'No, no, far from it. I'm from the same grateful department that long ago, with your help, made contact with Edward Avon in Paris,' he said, handing her a pocket-wallet with his photograph and signature as Stephen Pearson. She looked at the photograph, and then, for longer than he expected, at him. A nun's eyes: steadfast, innocent, devout.

'Is Edward –' She began again. 'He is well? He is not –'

'As far as I know, Edward's fine. It's his wife who's not well.'

'Deborah?'

'Yes. The same wife. This room's a bit large. Is there somewhere we can talk more privately?'

*

Her office was very cramped, with half an arched window of stained glass cut off by a partition wall, folding plastic chairs and an old trestle table for a desk. Uncertain what to do with him, she sat herself straight-backed at the table like a good schoolgirl and watched while he drew up a chair opposite her. Then in a gesture of truce she folded her hands together, which were long and sculpted and very graceful.

'So do you still see Edward from time to time?' Proctor asked.

Startled shake of the head.

'You don't mind if I call you Ania?'

'Of course not.'

'And I'm Stephen. And you don't mind if we dive straight in? When d'you think was the very last time you saw Edward?'

'It is many years. Please. Why are you asking this?'

'For no great reason, Ania. It's just that anybody who works for a secret department gets investigated now and then. Edward's turn has come round, that's all.'

'When he is so old? When he is not yours any more?'

'How do you know he's not ours?' – in the same gently humorous tone. 'Did he tell you he's no longer working for us? When might he have told you that? Do you remember?'

'He did not tell me. It was my assumption.'

'Based on what, I wonder?'

'I don't know. My expression was incidental. It was not material.'

'But you must remember, surely, when you last heard of him or saw him.'

Still nothing.

'Then let me help you. In March 1995 – a long while back, I know – at a little after midnight, Edward arrived at Gatwick Airport on a UNHCR flight from Belgrade in a dishevelled state, carrying nothing but his British passport. Does the date ring a bell, now?'

If it did, she gave no sign of it.

'He was in bad shape. He'd seen bad things. Atrocities. Murdered children. The horrors of the real world we all try to hide from, as he wrote not long ago to a friend of his.'

He paused to let this sink in, but without apparent effect.

'He needed someone he trusted. Somebody who cared about him and would understand. Does none of this come back to you?'

A lowering of the nun's eyes. An unfolding of the long hands. Receiving no other answer, he went on:

'He didn't try to get in touch with Deborah, who was anyway attending a conference in Tel Aviv. He didn't try to make contact with his daughter, who was at a West Country school for girls. So who did he turn to in his desperation?' Proctor mused, much as if he were speaking to an errant member of his own family. 'Until a few days ago, it was just another unsolved mystery. Even Edward himself didn't know where he'd been. It took him four days to report in to Head Office, and like everybody else he could only imagine that the strain of the last months in Bosnia had taken its toll and he had gone walkabout. However, modern technology being what it is, we have been able to recover certain old telephone records from that period. And they tell us a different story.'

He paused and glanced at her, waiting for a response, but the nun's eyes refused him.

'They tell us that somebody using a public telephone at

Gatwick Airport at one o'clock on the night he landed made a reverse-charge call to your flat in Highbury. Were you staying in your flat at that time?'

'It is possible.'

'Did you accept a reverse-charge call in the early hours of that morning – 18th March 1995?'

'It is possible.'

'It was a long conversation. Nine pounds and twenty-eight pence. A fortune in those days. Did Edward come to you that night? Ania, listen to me, please.'

Was she weeping? He saw no tears, but her head had not lifted and she was gripping the table so tightly that her thumbnails were white.

'Ania. I have to do this, all right? I'm not your enemy. Edward's a good, brave man. We both know that. But he's a lot of people. And if one of them's gone astray, we have to know that too and, if necessary, help him.'

'He has not gone astray!'

'I'm asking you whether Edward came to your flat that night almost twenty years ago. It's a simple question, yes or no? Did Edward, or did he not, come to your flat?'

She raised her head and looked him full in the face, and it was anger, not tears, that he saw.

'I have a companion, Mr Pearson,' she said.

'I'm aware of that.'

'His name is Felix.'

'I'm aware of that too.'

'Felix also is a good man.'

'I accept that.'

'Felix opened the front door to Edward. Felix paid his taxi

from Gatwick. Felix wished Edvard welcome in our house. Sorry, we have no spare bedroom in our house. For four days Edvard was sleeping on our sofa. Felix is a musicologist. He is committed to his students. Therefore he cannot disappoint them. Fortunately I have an assistant here at my school and was able to remain in our apartment as the nurse of Edvard.'

A delay while her anger subsided.

'Edvard was not well. He did not wish to have a doctor. I did not wish to leave him alone. On the fourth day Felix gave Edvard some clothes and took him to a barber to be shaved. On Monday he thanked us and said goodbye.'

'And in those four days he had made a miraculous recovery,' Proctor suggested, not without irony.

The suggestion annoyed her.

'What is recovered? When he left our house, Edvard was quiet. He was smiling. He was grateful. He was amusing. He was insincere again. He was Edvard. If that is recovered, yes, he was recovered, Mr Pearson.'

'But he wasn't recovered when he got to Head Office that same morning, was he? He had no idea where he'd been for four nights. He thought he'd got his new clothes from the Salvation Army. He wasn't even sure about that. He thought they might have given him a shave too. And he couldn't begin to understand where he'd got his bus ticket from. So why did he lie to us? Why are you lying to me now?'

'I don't know!' she shouted back. 'Go to hell. I am not your spy.'

Proctor's world swayed and righted itself. He had got it

straight now. It was Ellen who was lying to him, not Ania. He doubted whether Ania even had it in her to lie. If Ania was lying at all, it was only by omission. Not in her teeth. Not for the sheer hell of it, with her archaeological lover-boy grinning his face off on the bed beside her, if that's what he was doing.

*

'Was Edward a different man when he came to you both that night?' Proctor asked quietly.

'Maybe.'

'In what way?'

'I don't know. He was not different. He was committed. Edvard was always committed.'

'And he was committed to Salma?'

'Salma?' – in a feeble pretence of ignorance.

'The tragically bereaved woman in Bosnia he so admired. Mother of the murdered boy. Widow of the murdered doctor.'

Frowning, she affected unconvincingly to consult her memory. 'Maybe with Felix he spoke about this woman. With a man, maybe it was easier for him. He spoke many, many hours with Felix.'

'No. With Felix he spoke about how to save the world. We know that. So do you. They've been loyal pen friends ever since. With you he talked about Salma, surely. Something huge in his life had happened. Like the night in Paris when he told you he no longer believed in Communism. You would understand. Only you.'

'And Deborah, his wife?' she demanded. 'She would not understand him?'

But, like Proctor's, her anger couldn't last.

'He wished that he had died for her,' she said. 'He was ashamed. He would follow her to Jordan. She told him: go home to your wife, go home to your child, be a Western man. She was his passion. He was sick with her. She was not religious. She was wise. She was perfect. She was tragic. She was noble. Her family possessed the key to an ancient gate in the Holy City of Jerusalem. It was the Damascus Gate. Maybe Jaffa. I don't remember.'

Did Proctor catch a hint of impatience in her voice – even jealousy?

'She was also secret,' he proposed. 'Why did he have to keep her so secret from everyone, I wonder.'

'For Deborah.'

'To protect her feelings?'

'She was his wife.'

'But Salma was only an obsession, as you say. It wasn't a love-affair in the accepted sense. It was – what? Something a bit bigger, perhaps? A conversion? A sea-change that he didn't want anyone to know about. Not his wife, not his Service. Isn't that what he talked to Felix about?'

A different Ania. Her face locked tight as a castle door.

'Felix is a humanist. He is engaged. This you know very well, Mr Pearson. He has many important conversations with many people. I do not ask him what takes place.'

'Well, perhaps I'll ask him myself. Do you happen to know where I might get hold of him?'

'Felix is in Gaza.'
'So we gather. Give him our regards.'

*

From the top of a No. 113 bus, *en clair* text to Battenby, Vice Chief of the Service, ahead of this evening's meeting:

We may now safely assume target is conscious to our interest if he wasn't already.

Pearson

10

Deborah Avon was dead. Within hours of her passing, Julian had quietly assembled the salient facts.

At six in the evening Deborah's Macmillan nurse had summoned Lily to her mother's bedside. Deborah presented Lily with the rings from her fingers and asked her to fetch Edward, who was in his den.

On Edward's arrival, Deborah required both Lily and the nurse to leave her alone with her husband. Edward and Deborah remained cloistered in the bedroom with the door closed for fifteen minutes. Edward was then dismissed, apparently with instructions not to return.

It was then Lily's turn to sit alone with her mother while the nurse sat out of earshot on a chair in the corridor. Their conversation, according to Lily, took ten minutes, contents not disclosed to Julian. The nurse was readmitted. She and Lily remained in attendance to the end. By nine p.m. Deborah had entered a morphine-assisted coma. Around midnight her doctor certified life extinct.

Deborah's instructions relating to her death came into immediate effect. Her body was to be taken at once to a

Chapel of Rest, where it was to be viewed by nobody, repeat nobody. Lest there be any doubt on this score, her husband, Edward, was specifically named as unwelcome. To avoid misunderstanding, a copy of her letter of wishes had been lodged in advance with the undertaker.

Julian's own intimation of Deborah's death came with an imperious ring of the shop bell at six in the morning. Throwing on his dressing gown, he hurried downstairs to find Lily, dry-eyed, grim-jawed and speechless, standing on the doorstep.

His first fear, surprisingly in retrospect, was that something had happened to Sam. But then he reasoned that in that case she wouldn't be standing there staring at him, she'd be wherever Sam was. Later she told him that she'd ridden with her mother's body in the undertakers' van, but only as far as the chapel gates, in keeping with Deborah's instructions.

Guided by a sense of decorum that he afterwards could not explain to himself, Julian escorted her not to the intimacy of his flat but to Gulliver's coffee bar.

Though Lily and Sam had made flying visits to the shop during Deborah's final decline, they had never got as far as Gulliver's. Sam had taken one look at the funky staircase and let out a blood-curdling scream.

Lily's reaction at first sight of the coffee bar was little better:

'What utter crap!'

'What is?'

'Those fucking awful murals. Who did them?' – and, on being told a friend of Matthew: 'Well, she's bloody useless.'

'He, actually.'

'Then he's even worse,' she announced, hoisting herself on to a bar stool. 'Can you work that thing?' – jabbing a stubby finger at the coffee machine.

He could.

'I'll take a large cappuccino with extra chocolate. How much?'

Which was as far as she got before weeping her heart out in great sobs of pain. When Julian tried putting his arm round her, she shook him off and sobbed all the more. He made her a large cappuccino with extra chocolate but she ignored it. He gave her a glass of water, which she eventually drank.

'Where's Sam?' he asked her.

'Aunt Sophie's place.'

Aunt Sophie, Lily's old nanny, a wise Slav with a face like a battlefield.

'Where's Edward?'

She was speaking straight ahead of her in short, pithy sentences. Put together, they read as follows:

Edward and Deborah slept apart, the way they did everything else. After staring for some moments at her mother's body, Lily had called down the corridor for Edward. When he failed to emerge from his bedroom, she hammered on the door. 'Dad, Dad, she's dead.' He was freshly shaven. His sandalwood shaving soap. When had he shaved, she wondered. No tears on either side. He hugged her, she hugged him back. Then she got hold of his shoulders and rocked him to loosen him up, but he wouldn't loosen.

Then she got hold of his head in both hands and made

him look at her, which he'd tried not to do. And what she saw in his face, or thought she saw, wasn't grief, it was more like determination:

'I need to talk to you, Lily, he says. Talk away, I said. For Christ's sake, Dad, talk! Then he says: We'll talk this evening, Lily. Please make sure you're home for supper – like I was going to skive off to the fucking disco the night after my mum died.'

'And now?' Julian asked.

'Now he's taken the car off for one of his great long walks.'

For an hour or more after that, perched on her stool in Gulliver's, Lily did her mourning alone, now looking at herself in disbelief in the horizontal mirror behind the coffee machine, or glowering at the murals, while Julian intermittently kept a discreet watch on her. The last time he looked there was no Lily, and the cappuccino with extra chocolate was sitting untouched on the counter.

*

Next morning she was back, this time with Sam.

'So how was Edward?' Julian asked her.

'All right. Why?'

'I meant last night. You had a supper date with him. He wanted to talk to you.'

A vagueness came over her.

'Did he? Yeah, I suppose he did.'

'But nothing bad. Nothing drastic.'

'Drastic? Why should it be?' – mildly surprised, like her

father, to be asked the question, and at the same time turning it round.

And the 'keep out' sign firmly in place.

'So how does Edward spend his time otherwise?' he asked brightly, not quite changing the subject, but almost.

'Otherwise?'

'Yes.'

She shrugged. 'In his own cloud. Drifting round Mum's no-go area. Picking stuff up and putting it down.'

'No-go area?'

'Her lair. Fire-proof, bomb-proof, burglar-proof, family-proof. Semi-basement at the back of the house. All kitted out for her' – in the same grudging tone.

'Who by?'

'The fucking Secret Service, who do you suppose?'

*

Who did he suppose?

Well, in a vague way, he had supposed it for some while, without putting a name to it so bluntly. But had she inadvertently dropped her guard, or was she merely administering a slap-down for his inquisitiveness?

He was not inclined to ask. She was her father's child. Her reticence – not to say secrecy – was as much a part of her nature as it was of Edward's. And, as an only son who had grown to manhood with no sisters, Julian couldn't help regarding any relationship between father and daughter with a mixture of suspicion and awed respect.

If Lily had pulled the shutters down on her appointed

talk with her father, she was equally unforthcoming on her death-bed exchanges with her mother. Nevertheless Julian could not escape the impression that both conversations were in some sense officially classified. And this feeling was intensified when Lily casually announced that she wouldn't be coming to the shop that morning because she had to be at Silverview for when 'the men in brown overalls come to cart off Mum's wall safe and computer and shit'.

'What men, for heaven's sake?' Julian asked in unfeigned astonishment.

'Mum's men. Keep up, Julian! The people she worked for.'

'In her quango?'

'Yeah, right, got it. Her quango. The Men from the Quango. Title of my next book.'

*

It isn't until the arrangements for the funeral begin to take shape that the last of Lily's cover, if such it is, crumbles. The scene is Gulliver's, which Lily, despite its awful murals, has appointed her field headquarters. The date, four days after Deborah's death. Sam's horror of the funky staircase has vanished from the day Julian hoisted him on his shoulders and marched him up the steps to the strains of 'The Grand Old Duke of York'. Sam and Matthew have hit it off from the start. Sometimes Milton, Deborah's former carer, will wander in and, with a wave to the company, settle himself languidly on the floor, and Sam and Milton will do animal jigsaws with scarcely a word passing between them.

But this lunchtime, it's just Julian and Lily and Sam. Sam

has taken all the children's books from their shelves and is spreading them over the floor. Julian has just come back from fetching sandwiches and Lily is deep in conversation on her cellphone:

'Yeah, got it. Okay, Honour . . . Sure . . . yeah, whatever it takes . . .' and, as soon as she has rung off, or possibly just before: 'Fuck her.'

'Fuck who? Whom?' Julian asks lightly.

'It's all fixed. Ask Honour. We don't have to do a bloody thing any more. It's tomorrow week, twelve midday, and a knees-up at the Royal Haven to follow. Mum wanted a Saturday so that her old Service pals can show up, so it's a Saturday.' And remembering: 'Oh, yeah, and by the way, Dad wants you to be his best man.'

'His what?'

'Pallbearer. Whatever the fuck. I'm not up in this stuff, all right? Nor's Dad. So it's not easy, right?'

'I'm not suggesting it is.'

'Good,' Lily retorts, sounding this time more like her mother than her father.

'So who's Honour?' Julian asks, and, to his surprise, given Lily's fighting mood, she falls quiet for a while.

'We're spies, right? Mum's one, Dad's another, and I'm their go-between.' And with a resurgence of outrage: 'And it's fucking sick' – driving her clenched fist on to the stainless steel counter. 'Mum lived her whole fucking life under wraps. They wouldn't even let her wear her fucking medal on Remembrance Day, but as soon as she's dead they want to float her down the fucking Thames on the Royal Barge with the Brigade of Guards playing "Abide With Me".'

Bit by bit, the rest came out. Within hours of Deborah's death, it seemed, Honour had introduced herself to Lily, first by cellphone then by email. Honour's speciality was Service funerals, and she wanted to put Deborah's funeral on hold while she mustered the clans – her phrase. Lily took particular exception to the way Honour spoke, which she compared to Margaret Thatcher with a potato stuck in her gullet.

Honour had now done her mustering, which was what the call had been about. On present count, she anticipated a turnout of fifty to sixty past and present members and their partners. The Service would be happy to stand two-thirds of the cost of the reception, which the Royal Haven was putting at nineteen quid a guest to include canapés from Menu C, red and white wine and a catering staff of six. A Senior Official would deliver an address of not more than twelve minutes in length.

'And does our Senior Official have a name, or shouldn't I ask?' Julian enquires facetiously.

'Harry Knight,' Lily replies, and, doing her Honour voice: 'As in shining armour, dear.'

And Edward? How was Edward taking to Honour's ministrations?

'Dad's totally out of it. Whatever Mum wanted is all right by him. So don't ask him' – with the usual 'keep out' signs.

As a mark of her grief, she has taken to wearing the *Doctor Zhivago* scarf yanked forward around her face, making herself unrecognisable except from the front.

*

The days crept uneasily by. In the afternoons Lily and Sam would go down to the playground or walk beside the river, and if the bookshop were quiet Julian would tag along. Sometimes Aunt Sophie would turn up unannounced and take Sam off on a jaunt: Sophie who, in Lily's words, had 'worked with Dad abroad in some weird capacity'. But Julian knew better than to ask. He was learning to see the entire Avon clan and its offshoots as being united, not in the secrets they shared, but in the secrets they kept from one another: a concept that rang bells from his own childhood.

But, although it took him a while to realise it, Lily was quietly talking her way out of prison.

Early evening, sun after rain. Julian and Lily sauntering hand in hand along the footpath. Julian assuming her mind is with Deborah. Sam and Aunt Sophie out ahead of them.

'Know what my pad in Bloomsbury was before I got it?'

A bordello? – facetiously. She hoots.

'A Service safe house, idiot! When it wasn't safe any more, they let Mum buy it at cost as a favour. So Mum gave it to us. Great, but we couldn't move in for a month. Why not? Go on. Guess!'

Rising damp? Rats? Cheque bounced?

'Because we'd got to wait till the sweepers had given it the green light.'

To her delight, Julian falls straight in, perhaps deliberately.

'Not fucking cleaners, idiot! Sweepers. Sweeping it for bugs. Electronic listening devices to you. They weren't putting them in. They'd done that already. They were pulling them out. I keep hoping to find one they've missed, so I can talk dirty into it.'

But it's her laughter that he enjoys the most, and the feel of her arm slung round his waist, and the way it stays there when she turns pensive again.

'Local rumour has it that Deborah and Edward had a falling out over your grandfather's collection of blue-and-white porcelain,' Julian throws in once, risking a probe.

'News to me.' She shrugs. 'Mum said she was sick of the sight of the stuff, and they'd put it into store to save the insurance.'

And Dad? Best not to ask.

And when Julian lets drop that somebody mentioned to him that Chinese blue-and-white porcelain had been Edward's passion in his retirement:

'Passion? Dad wouldn't know his Ming from his elbow,' she scoffs.

As to fallings out between her parents, all Lily knows is – mainly from Aunt Sophie, who was helping in the house at the time – that there'd been a screaming match 'in Mum's lair', which Edward theoretically wasn't supposed to enter because of need-to-know. But Lily is sceptical: Sophie wasn't always the most reliable source.

'If anyone screamed, it was Mum. Dad never screamed in his life. Sophie thought Dad must have swiped her, but Dad doesn't do that either. So maybe Mum swiped him. Or maybe it never happened.'

'Have you been in there?'

'The lair? Once. You can have one little peep, darling, and that's all you get ever. Great, I say. You do in-trays, you do a green phone on a red stand, you do industrial-sized computers. What else do you do, Mum? Protect our country from its enemies, darling. As I hope you will one day.'

'And Edward?' Julian asks. 'Who does he protect us from?'

Wait while she decides how much to tell him.

'Dad?'

'Yes. Dad.'

'Special work. That was all they told me when they took me out to lunch. I tried Mum. What was Dad doing in Bosnia while I was at boarding school? Aid work, darling. Plus a little of this and that. What the fuck's this and that? I said. Don't swear, darling.'

'Did you ask your dad direct?'

'Not really.'

*

And probably it was only natural that, in the process of liberating herself from her secrets, Lily should keep her most disturbing revelation until last.

'And Mum made me take a letter to London for her,' she broke out, over a lager in The Fisherman's Rest. 'Safe house in South Audley Street. Ring three times and ask for Proctor.'

At which point, Julian might have replied that he too had delivered a confidential letter, not for her mother but her father. But if the solemn promise he'd made to Edward hadn't held him back, his concern for Lily would have done. With Deborah's funeral three days away, this was no time to be telling her that her father had been conducting a long-term relationship with a beautiful woman who had no name.

'Anyway, I've told him now, haven't I?' she said defiantly. 'Did you deliver a letter for your mother? Yes, I did. Was it to Proctor? Yes, it bloody was. Did you know what was in it? No, I bloody didn't and Proctor asked me the same question. Then he hugged me and said it was all right, I'd done the right thing and so had he.'

'Proctor had?'

'Dad had, for Christ's sake! Gave me his papal blessing. Standing in front of the drawing-room fire that's never lit: go forth in peace, my darling, your mother was a fine woman, I did what I had to do, and I'm only sorry that she and I inhabited different universes.'

'But what did he do that he had to do?'

The door closing on him again.

'They just had different secrets,' she said curtly.

*

My dear Julian,

You will forgive me if, in these difficult circumstances, I have not responded sooner to your kind messages of condolence. Deborah will indeed be a great loss to those who loved her. Let me say also how touched I am that you are sharing with Lily the burden of the funeral arrangements, which in better circumstances would fall on my shoulders. Might you nonetheless find time for an hour or two's refreshing walk tomorrow afternoon? The weather promises well. I suggest three p.m., and attach a map for your convenience.

Edward

'Orford?' Matthew echoed in horror when Julian chanced to mention his destination. 'Well, if you like war zones.'

★

The day is radiant as only the end of spring can be. There is promise of rain but no sign of it in the whole blue sky. Julian's venerable Land Cruiser – not as much fun as the Porsche he has renounced, but good for ferrying books about – enables him to see over hedgerows at new-born lambs taking their first tottering steps into life. For twenty miles and more he passes through groomed countryside with barely a house or human being to disturb the idyll. Daffodils and fruit blossom evoke memories of country vicarages before his father's fall.

The prospect of meeting Edward is a relief to him. For days now the aid worker of Bosnia, secret lover, spy and seemingly unrepentant widower has been a phantom figure for him, patrolling the ill-lit corridors of Silverview like Hamlet's father, scarcely speaking to his daughter and disappearing without notice on mysterious walks.

An ancient three-towered castle appeared on his right side. His satnav guided him into a prinked-up village square, down a slip road to an inland quay. A large empty car park was darkened by tall trees. As he parked, a new version of Edward stepped out of their shadow: Edward the outdoor man, in waxed green jacket, battered hat and walker's boots.

'Edward, I'm just so very sorry,' Julian said, shaking his hand.

'You are kind, Julian,' Edward replied in a distracted tone. 'Deborah regarded you highly.'

They set out. Julian had no need of Matthew's dire warning. He had battled his way through *Rings of Saturn*. He knew what to expect of the godforsaken loneliness of that outpost in the middle of nowhere. He knew that even fishermen supposedly found it unbearable. They followed a pedestrian walk past rubbish bins, climbed a rickety wooden stairway, and waded through a mess of mud and ships' junk to emerge on a littered quayside.

Edward struck out left. The river wall forced them into single file. Pebbles of rain whipped off the sea. Edward swung round in his tracks.

'We are famous for our bird life here, actually, Julian,' he announced, with proprietorial pride. 'We have lapwing, curlew, bittern, meadow pipit, avocets, not to mention duck,' he declared, like a headwaiter reciting the day's specials. 'Look now, please. You hear that curlew calling to her mate? Follow my arm.'

Julian made a show of doing so, but for some minutes he had been able to follow only the horizon: the remains of our own civilisation after its destruction in some future catastrophe. And there they stood: distant forests of abandoned aerials rising out of the mist, abandoned hangars, barracks, accommodation blocks and control rooms, pagodas on elephantine legs for stress-testing atom bombs, with curved roofs but no walls in case the worst happens. And, at his feet, a warning to him to stick to marked paths or reckon with unexploded ordnance.

'You are moved by this hellish place, Julian?' Edward enquired, observing his distraction. 'I too.'

'Is that why you come here?'

'Yes, it is,' he replied with unusual candour. And, taking Julian's arm, a thing he had never done before: 'Listen hard. Do you listen? Now tell me what you hear above the screaming of the birds.' And when Julian heard nothing but more screams and the skirmishing of the wind: 'How about the rumble of the guns of our glorious British past? No? No guns?'

'What do you hear?' Julian asked awkwardly, with a laugh to dispel the severity of Edward's stare.

'I?' – as ever, surprised to be asked. 'Why, the guns of our glorious future. What else?'

What else indeed, Julian wondered. And wondered it all the more when, reaching the end of a sand bar, Edward again took his arm, guided him to a makeshift bench of driftwood and sat down beside him.

'It occurs to me that we may not get a chance to speak alone for a while,' he announced brusquely.

'Why on earth not?'

'After a funeral, many things change. There will be new imperatives. New lives must be led. I cannot be the shop's parasitic house guest indefinitely.'

'Parasitic?'

'With poor Deborah no longer with us, I shall have no excuse.'

'You don't need an excuse, Edward. You're welcome any time. We're building a great library together, remember?'

'I do remember, and you have been most generous and

I am ashamed to have trespassed on your hospitality, but it was unfortunately necessary.' Necessary? 'Our Republic is well founded. It requires only your proven administrative skills to bring it to fruition. I shall be superfluous. My friend thought well of you.'

'Mary?'

'She had no fear that you were betraying me. She was happy to entrust you with her reply to my letter. She remarked that you were a man of integrity. She is a woman with great experience of the real world.'

'Is she all right?'

'Thank you, she is safe, I am pleased to say.'

'Well, good on Mary.'

'Exactly.'

The conversation had stopped: on Julian's side for want of words; on Edward's because he was mustering his thoughts.

'And you have an affection for my daughter, I observe. You are not deceived by her volatile stance on occasions?'

'Should I be?

'Lily, I venture to say, is not naturally given to concealing her emotions.'

'Maybe she's had too many other things to conceal,' Julian ventured.

'And Sam is not a hindrance?'

'Sam? He's an asset.'

'He will rule the world one day.'

'Let's hope so. You're not telling me to marry her, are you?'

'Oh, my dear fellow, nothing so fatal' – Edward's face

briefly lighting into a smile. 'I merely needed to be assured that Lily's affections were not misplaced. You have provided me with that assurance.'

'Are you going somewhere, Edward? What is this?'

Could that have been a flash of alarm in Edward's face? A second glance convinced Julian that he had been mistaken, for Edward's features reflected nothing but a whimsical sadness:

'I am in the past now, Julian. I can do no harm. I wish you to know that, if occasion arises, you are free to discuss me. There are people we must never betray, whatever the cost. I do not belong in that category. I have no claim on you. I loved your father. Now give me your hand. So. When we return to the car park I shall say only a formal farewell to you.'

First it was the strong hand. Then it was an impulsive embrace, one side only, then let go before they see us.

II

For the second time in as many weeks Julian was dressing for Deborah, but today he had no doubts about whether to wear his dark City suit. In his shaving mirror he could see the medieval church standing proud on the hill. The flag of St George flew at half-mast from its spire. At its foot lay the ancient seafarers' graveyard from which, according to legend, their spirits could go back to sea.

I have spent my life adhering to the superstitions of my tribe, and I intend to be buried according to its rituals.

Lily had ordered him to be on parade by eleven fifteen. Neither at his father's funeral nor his mother's had he been a pallbearer. The playfully gruesome prospect that he might trip up or make a mess of it had featured now and then in his many conversations with Lily and throughout most of the night.

Silverview gave her the creeps.

Edward loved her so much he couldn't get it together to speak to her. Five minutes, and he was out of the door.

Even Sam's gone quiet. She's moved him into her bedroom and finally, finally, he's nodded off.

Love you, Jules. Sleep well.

Ten minutes later, she's back. Or she texts him. Or he calls her.

After heavy rain the day dawned clear. His City shoes notwithstanding, Julian decided to walk. As he climbed the hill, the monotonous tolling of the church bell grew louder, summoning not just the townspeople but the estimated fifty to sixty past and present members predicted by Honour. The car park was a mass of brown puddles that the church couldn't afford to fill. To park in it was to risk wet feet and muddy shoes. Two sycophantic police officers were urging arrivals to ignore yellow lines. At the church porch, mourners were greeting and embracing. A couple of men in suits were handing out Orders of Service. Under a spreading cypress tree a trio of young undertakers were having a discreet fag. He was assailed by Celia, all in black. A small man in a camel-hair coat and orange pigskin gloves hovered at her elbow.

'You haven't met my Bernard, have you, young Mr Julian?' Celia demanded in a barbed voice, at the same time fixing him with a steely glare. 'Maybe we could have a little talk after. Yes?' What the hell was that about?

Two volunteer ladies from the library seized him:

'Isn't it awful?'

Awful, he agreed.

Next came Ollie the butcher and his partner, George.

'You haven't seen Lily around, by any chance?' he asked.

'In the vestry with Vicar,' said George promptly.

'Now you're the bookseller,' a tall, strong-faced woman informed him. 'I'm Deborah's cousin Leslie. And I'm looking for Lily too. And this is my husband.'

How d'you do.

The vestry door stood open. Cope-chest. Rush crosses on the wall. The incense of his childhood but no Vicar and no Lily. He kept going and found her standing in a patch of deep grass, between two vast buttresses, a Victorian waif in a black cloche hat and a long skirt. At her feet, a small mountain of red wreaths and flowers.

'I've said to put them round the grave,' she said.

'Then they go up to the hospital. Did you tell them that?'

'No.'

'I will. Get any sleep?'

'No. Hug me.'

He did.

'The undertakers should make a list of the labels in case they come adrift. I'll tell them that too. Where's Sam?'

'With Milton, down the playground. I'm not having him anywhere near.'

'Edward?'

'Inside the church.'

'Doing what?'

'Staring at the fucking wall.'

'Do I leave you here, or d'you want to join the throng?'

'Behind you.'

It was a warning. A tall, rugger-playing man with a gritted smile had bounded up to him:

'Hi. I'm Reggie. Devoted colleague of Debbie's. You're Julian, yes? Bookseller? We're co-pallbearers. Good. Follow me.'

A few yards off, four more Reggies and a portly

undertaker with a top hat under his arm stood waiting. Mute handshakes. Hi. Hi. The undertaker requires a few uninterrupted words, gentlemen, if he may:

'I will commence with an admonition, gentlemen. Do not on any account touch the handles. If you touch the handles, you will find yourselves going home with them. It's one shoulder apiece, and one hand each for our departed and I personally shall give the off, and I shall be with you every step of the way in the unlikely event of a mishap. And kindly mind the third flagstone, it's a shocker. Worries at all, gentlemen?'

'The family want the flowers sent up to the general hospital tomorrow morning, and they'd like a list of the labels,' Julian said.

'Thank you, sir, and that is all attended to as per contract. Further questions? In that case, I will ask that we proceed to the porch to await the arrival of the hearse.'

An older woman leapt at Julian and embraced him.

'Do you realise? The whole of F7 has turned out!' she announced excitedly. 'And some people who simply never go to funerals. Isn't that absolutely marvellous?'

'It's great,' Julian agreed.

*

Slow-marching up the aisle, watching out for the third flagstone, one hand for our departed and one-sixth of her bodyweight pressing on his right shoulder, Julian takes stock of the congregation, starting with Lily, who sits front left in the north aisle next to her father. Of Edward he sees only a pair of smartly suited shoulders and the back of his white head.

Honour's fifty-to-sixty-strong contingent is divided into two groups, he decides: past members to front pews in the main aisle, present members to rear pews in the south aisle, where they can see and not be seen. Coincidence? Or deft work by Service ushers? He suspects the second.

Two carved fruitwood angels kneel either side of the crimson altar. A coffin table stands before it. To a whispered command of 'Down' from the undertaker, the biodegradable coffin containing the mortal remains of Deborah Avon is laid faultlessly on the table. As he stoops with it, Julian glimpses a gold medal with a green ribbon nestling among the red roses on the lid. A bald organist in his mirror strikes up a mournful Voluntary. Turning in time with his fellow bearers, Julian takes his place at Lily's side. Her gloved hand finds his, curls and nestles familiarly inside his palm. She whispers 'Jesus' and closes her eyes. On her far side, Edward stares sightlessly ahead of him, chin up, shoulders back, as he faces the firing squad.

*

Looking tiny and unprotected at the lectern, Lily in her cloche hat and black skirt reads a poem by Kipling, her mother's choice. For once, her voice is so faint that it reaches no further than the first couple of pews.

A violent blast of organ music is the starting signal for fifty to sixty past and present members and their partners to spring to their feet as one. The townsfolk clamber after them. The wagon roof trembles as the congregation in thunderous unison pledges itself to labour night and day to be a pilgrim. The music fades and Harry Knight is standing in the pulpit.

Whatever Harry's name may be, he is perfectly cast. Whatever the Service stands for, he stands for it. He is plain-spoken, wholesome and forthright. There is an air of lightly borne moral rectitude about him. He keeps both hands visible at all times, and speaks fluently without benefit of notes.

Deborah's rare personal beauty, her wit.

The sad early loss of her mother.

Her good fortune to be brought up in the shadow of her father, soldier, scholar, art collector, philanthropist.

Her love of country.

Her determination to put duty before self.

Her love of family, the support she derived from her devoted husband.

Her unmatched linguistic gifts. Her clarity of intellect. Her rare powers of analysis.

Her love above all of service. Of the Service.

Are the townspeople asking themselves how all these rare talents were invested in the woman they have distantly known as some kind of committee person? It seems they aren't. Julian sees no puzzlement in their rapt faces. Even when Harry Knight reads out a personal message from the Chief of the exclusive firm for which dear Deborah laboured so tirelessly for so many years, their response is only of vague rapture.

Another hymn.

Endless prayers.

All Julian's childhood coming back to get him.

The Vicar sports a row of medal ribbons. Is he a local hero, or does he work the same circuit as Harry Knight and Honour? Today's collection will be in aid of Church Missions abroad. To spare our overworked volunteers, will mourners kindly replace hymnals and psalters neatly on the lower shelf of the pew in front of you as you leave? The interment will follow immediately, family and invited guests only, please. The rest of the congregation is invited to proceed to the Royal Haven Hotel two hundred yards down the hill. Anybody with food allergies, please inform the catering staff. Disabled facilities available. As the organ enters a mood of languorous despair, Julian and his fellow pallbearers reassemble at their places round the coffin and, led by the portly undertaker, slow-march it to the waiting hearse, then seat themselves awkwardly in the car behind it for a round-about journey between roadworks down a red clay track. The Vicar and a half-dozen family mourners have been bussed ahead. The pallbearers alight. The younger under takers shuffle out the coffin, the pallbearers re-form. Lily and Edward are standing several yards back from the grave's edge. Lily is clutching Edward's arm in a lock-grip, her fingers linked and white. As a further reminder to him of her presence, she has propped her head on his shoulder.

He said Mum didn't want him at her graveside. I said, if he didn't come, I wouldn't. What the fuck did they do to each other, Jules? Lily marvels drowsily into his cellphone in the small hours of this morning.

To a series of commands from the portly undertaker, the

six pallbearers halt, hesitate, then slowly ease the coffin from their shoulders – the tricky bit – transfer it to their hands and gingerly lower it on to the wooden slats, then grasp the webs while the lesser undertakers remove the slats. And so consign Deborah to her resting place.

'Marvellous send-off,' Reggie remarks, coming alongside Julian as they head down the hill to the Royal Haven. 'Just what she deserved. And poor Edward bearing up pretty well, don't you think? All things considered?'

And what are they exactly, Julian wonders.

*

They were latecomers. The family only had yet to arrive.

'Now we should know each other but we don't,' Harry Knight complained heartily as they shook hands.

And, when Julian gave his name: 'Of course I know who you are! Friend of Edward, friend of the family. Good to have you.'

'And I'm Honour,' said a pleasantly vague woman in a mauve shawl. 'And Lily says you've been a quite wonderful support.'

A huddle of townspeople had gathered at the far end of the assembly room. Out of them strode Celia, closely attended by Bernard in his camel-hair coat.

'I'd like my quiet word with you, young Mr Julian, if you can spare a moment,' she said, seizing his arm in no very friendly way. 'All right. Tell me. Who've you been talking to?'

'Just now?'

'Don't just now me. Who've you bubbled to about my

grande collection and certain informal rewards I've been receiving on the side?'

'Celia. For Christ's sake. Why on earth should I have bubbled to anyone?'

'What about those rich City friends of yours you were going to keep an ear out for?'

'We left it that if I ever heard anything, I'd tell you. I haven't heard anything. And I haven't spoken to anyone. Does that satisfy you?'

'It doesn't satisfy Her Majesty's Value Added Tax Inspectors, I'll tell you that for nothing. Barging into my emporium like the heavy mob. "We have reason to believe, Mrs Merridew, that you have been receiving back-pocket payments by way of commission on certain undeclared transactions in blue-and-white porcelain over a large number of years, and we are accordingly seizing your account books and your computer forthwith and immediately." Whoever told them that, then? Not Teddy. He wouldn't.'

The rat-like face of Bernard appeared at Celia's shoulder:

'Only I told her to go to the police, didn't I, but she won't,' he complained. 'Not the police. She never will, will you?'

A subdued flurry signalled the late arrival of the family, with Edward still on Lily's arm. Julian was about to make his way to her when he was again cornered by the energetic Reggie, who until now had been lavishing his charm on the unattended guests.

'Mind if I grab you for a moment, Julian?'

He had already done so. They were standing in a recess

leading to the kitchen, with catering staff sweeping past them with trays of wine and canapés.

'A senior colleague of mine needs very much to talk to you,' Reggie said. 'It's got to be now-ish, I'm afraid.'

'About what?'

'Security of the realm. He's checked you out, got a high regard for you. Is Paul Overstrand a name?'

'He gave me my first City job. Why?'

'Paul sends his best regards. Jerry Seaman, your former fellow director?'

'What about him?'

'Says you're a shit, but your heart's in the right place. I'm parked round the corner in Carter Street. Black BMW. With a red K in the windscreen. Got that? Carter Street. Black BMW, red K. Give me five minutes, then follow me out. Tell them Matthew thinks he's having a heart attack or something.'

Tradesmen, spies and local gentry were getting to know each other. Edward and Lily stood at the entrance, Lily with her glass held wide, embracing people unselectively, Edward mute and upright, shaking any hand that was offered him. Of past and present members, only a smattering seemed to know him.

'They want to talk to me,' Julian said, guiding Lily aside. 'They want me to make up some stupid excuse. I'm just going to fade. I'll call you as soon as I can.'

And as a spontaneous afterthought:

'I don't think you should tell your father.'

Stepping into the street, he was greeted by two of the other pallbearers, who fell in beside him for the fifty-yard walk to Carter Street. The black BMW was parked on a double yellow line. A policeman stood ten yards from it, studiously looking the other way. Reggie sat at the wheel. Behind it was a green Ford. As they set off, the green Ford pulled out behind them with the two pallbearers up front. Soon they were in open country.

'So what's his name?' Julian asked.

'Whose?'

'Your colleague's?'

'Smith, I should think. Got your cellphone handy?'

'Why?'

'Mind if I have it?' – holding out his left hand. 'Company regs, I'm afraid. You get it back at the end.'

'I think I'll hang on to it, if it's all the same to you,' Julian said.

Indicating left, Reggie drew into a convenient parking bay. Behind them, the green Ford did the same.

'So let's just play that again,' Reggie suggested.

Julian handed him his cellphone. They left the main road and took small, empty lanes. The sky had darkened. Big spots of rain splashed on to the windscreen. On their right lay an unmade track, marked by a 'For Sale' sign with SOLD pasted across it. They bounced over potholes, the green Ford following, and entered a large tumbledown settlement of partly thatched barns and mouldering labourers' cottages. At its centre stood a derelict farmhouse, faced with flaking weatherboard; and, around it, partly under shelter, an array of vehicles of every kind, ranging from middle-level cars and a tour coach to motorbikes, pushbikes, mopeds and perambulators, and – most notably to Julian's eye – a battered van, the very one, if he was not mistaken, that had accommodated a pair of passionate lovers on the lane to Silverview.

And here and there, leaving and entering the cottages, or tinkering with their cars or motorbikes, an equally varied assortment of mankind, from middle-aged couples to back-packers to a postman in uniform to mothers with their children. But what struck Julian, if anything, was their collective ordinariness, and how not a head turned to look at him as Reggie marched him towards the farmhouse, and a stalky man in a bland grey suit came picking his way gingerly down the broken steps, smiling his embarrassment and holding out his hand in welcome.

'Julian. Hullo. Stewart Proctor is my name. Sorry about the hijacking, but I'm afraid it's rather pressing national business.'

*

If Julian hadn't spoken, it wasn't for want of words or indignation, but because he realised belatedly that for days now, perhaps weeks, he had been waiting for some kind of resolution. They had left Reggie standing at the door. By the light of an old fashioned silver hand torch, Proctor led the way through the darkening house, over broken tiles and bare joists, through smashed French windows, to a circle of overgrown garden. In the middle stood a wooden summer house with its door open. A path had been cut through the long grass. A lighted oil lamp hung from the ceiling. On a ceramic table, Scotch, ice, soda and two tumblers.

'Couple of hours maximum unless anything goes seriously wrong,' Proctor announced, pouring two shots and handing him one. 'Then we'll have you run back into town. The subject for discussion, as I think you will have guessed, is Edward Avon, and its official classification is top secret and beyond. So, first of all, sign here, if you're willing, then forever after hold your peace' – proffering a printed form and, from the inside pocket of his suit, a ballpoint pen.

'If I'm not willing?' Julian asked.

'The roof falls in. We have you arrested on suspicion of providing aid and comfort to the Queen's enemies, and we produce the basement computer as evidence. You bonded together, you colluded, you conspired. You used the classics library for cover. They'd probably want to arrest poor Matthew as an accessory. Much better to sign. We need you.'

Julian picked up the pen and, with a shrug, signed the form unread.

'You seem less surprised than you ought to be,' Proctor said, taking back his pen and folding the form into his pocket. 'Did you have your suspicions?'

'Of what?'

'Did you and Edward ever discuss priceless Chinese porcelain?'

'No.'

'There used to be a collection of it at Silverview.'

'So I gather.'

'If I said Amsterdam Bont to you, you wouldn't know what I was talking about?'

'Not from Adam.'

'Batavia ware?'

'Also.'

'Imari? Kendi? Kraak? No, obviously. Would it then surprise you to know that these and similar terms have been
issuing in large numbers from your computer before being
doubly erased?'

'It would.'

'But not, presumably, that your Republic of Literature
and Celia's Bygones have priceless Chinese porcelain in
common?'

'Not now, no,' Julian replied impassively.

'On a slightly happier note, would it help to say that you
and I personally are concerned for his daughter, Lily, who,
as we both know, is blameless?'

'Go on.'

'Apart from providing Edward Avon with a sanctuary, a
computer and a cover story, did you ever do him any special
favours – run any errands for him – that in retrospect you
might wonder about – in the larger context, as it were?'

'Why should I have done?'

'Well, why's a separate question, isn't it? We searched your
flat, obviously, while you were out on one of your morning
runs. And came on this' – handing Julian a photographic
facsimile of his pocket diary. 'If you could turn to the page
for 18th April this year, you'll find you've jotted down the
registration number of a London minicab. Got it?'

He had.

'On the same page, there's a train time written down.
Ipswich to LS, seven forty-five a.m. LS, I take it, for
Liverpool Street. Were you in London that day?'

'Looks as though I must have been.'

'Not must. I suspect you volunteered out of the goodness of your heart. The minicab whose number you noted down – we'll come to why in a minute – was on account. It picked up one lady passenger from the premises of a regular client in the West End, drove her to Belsize Park, waited for her for twenty-seven minutes, and returned her to the West End. For your information, the journey was charged to the League of Arab States in Green Street. The cost was seventy-four pounds including waiting time and tip. Who was she?'

'I don't know.'

'Where did you meet her?'

'The Everyman Cinema, Belsize Park.'

'The driver confirms that. And from there?'

'The café next door. Brasserie.'

'Also confirmed. The meeting was at Edward's behest, I take it.'

A nod.

'Did you have personal business of your own that day?'

'No.'

'So a dedicated journey, also at Edward's behest, done as an act of charity at short notice. Am I right?'

'Asked me one day; I went the next.'

'Because it was so pressing? – so urgent for him?'

'Yes.'

'Why? Did he say?'

'It was urgent. He'd known her a long time. She was big in his life. It mattered to him. His wife was dying. I liked him. Still do.'

'But no indication of the role she might be playing in his life? Or has played?'

'He was mad about her. That was the implication.'

'What was her name?'

'None supplied. Mary for convenience.'

Proctor did not seem surprised.

'And the reason for this urgency?'

'None asked, none given.'

'And the contents of the letter? Its purpose. Message?'

'Ditto.'

'And you weren't tempted to read it at any point? You weren't. Good.'

Why good? Boy Scouts' honour? Probably, from the look of the man, yes.

'But Mary, as you call her, read the letter in front of you. According to the waitress, whom you tipped so handsomely.'

'Mary read it. I didn't.'

'Was it a long letter?'

'What does the waitress say?'

'What do you say?'

'Six sides of Edward's handwriting. Give or take.'

'And you rushed off and bought her stationery and laid it before her. And Sellotape. And then?'

'And then she wrote a letter.'

'Which you also didn't read, I assume. Addressed to Edward.'

'She didn't address it. She just gave me the plain envelope and said give it to him.'

'So why did you write down the number of her car?'

'Impulse. She was impressive. Special, in some way. I suppose I wanted to know more about her.'

'If you turn to the opposite page of your diary – for 17th April, the whole of it – you'll see you scribbled a note to yourself, I suspect on the journey back to Ipswich. Got it there?'

He was looking at it.

'Your note reads: "I am well, I am composed, I am at peace." Whose words are they?'

'Mary's.'

'Spoken to you by Mary?'

'Yes.'

'About herself, presumably.'

'Presumably.'

'What were you to do with them?'

'Pass them on to Edward. It would cheer him up. It did. He loved it. I told him she was beautiful. He loved that too. She was,' he added, from deep inside his thoughts.

'This beautiful?' Proctor asked, fishing a photograph album from under his chair, opening it and offering it to Julian across the ceramic-topped table.

A leggy blonde woman in a leopard-skin coat was stepping out of a limousine.

'More beautiful' – handing back the album.

'This?' – handing it back again.

Mary a few years ago. Mary with a black-and-white keffiyeh round her neck. Mary at a rostrum, addressing an open-air Arab crowd. Mary happy, with her fist raised. The crowd celebrating. Flags of many nations. The Palestinian flag prominent.

'He said she was safe,' Julian said.

'When did he tell you that?'

'Couple of days back. Walking at Orford. Where he likes to go.'

The silence again.

'What will you tell Lily?' Proctor asked.

'About what?'

'What we've just talked about. What you've seen. What her father is. Or was.'

'I've just signed my life away, haven't I? Why should I tell her anything?'

'But you will. So what will you tell her?'

Julian had been asking himself the same question for some while.

'I think, one way or another, Edward's pretty much told her,' he said.

*

Julian had forgotten that he had given Lily a key to the shop, and that a key to his flat was attached to it. He therefore took a moment to accept, when he switched on the light, that she was lying naked on his bed, that she was not a dream, and that she was holding her arms out to him like a drowning woman while the tears streamed down her cheeks.

'I thought it was time we showed a bit of respect for the living,' she confided to him, some time later.

12

'So they got you into the back of a Service Jag at last,' Battenby said, with half an eye for Proctor and the other half for a computer screen that Proctor couldn't see. 'Must be a first,' he mused in the same expressionless voice.

'Frightened the living daylights out of me,' Proctor confessed. 'A hundred and five on the A12, if you please. Not my scene.'

'Children flourishing?' Battenby enquired – another touch for the computer.

'Very much so, thanks, Quentin. Yours?'

'Yes, all very pleasing' – another touch. 'Ah, Teresa's in the lift now. She's been taking soundings.'

'Oh, fine,' said Proctor.

Soundings where? Teresa, formidable head of the Service's Legal Department, she who brooks no argument, is on her way up to the top floor, armed for battle.

They were seated in Battenby's top-floor office, just the two of them, Battenby at his bare desk, Proctor in a black leather armchair that squeaked when he sat down. The walls were nicely panelled in senior-directors-grade burr elm. By the low light, the black knots resembled bullet holes.

Quentin Battenby in the prime of middle age. He's been there ever since Proctor has known him. Swept-back blond hair, now at last greying. Understated film-star looks. Good suits, never takes his jacket off. Hasn't taken it off now. Never been heard to raise his voice; owns or is owned by a presentable wife who knows everyone's name at Service functions and is otherwise unseen. Bachelor flat across the river. House in St Albans where he and his family live under another name. Apolitical, but tipped to be in line for Chief provided he plays his cards right and the Tories win the next election. No close friends within the Service, therefore no close enemies. First-rate committee man. Parliamentary oversight people eat out of his hand.

If that was the sum of general knowledge about him, Proctor, who had been his running mate for twenty-five years, had little to add to it. Battenby's celestial rise had been an object of mystification to Proctor ever since he had known him. They were of the same age, same year, same intake. They had attended the same training courses, rubbed shoulders on the same operations, competed for the same appointments and promotions, until somehow Battenby had eased ahead of him, gradually and always effortlessly, and only recently in leaps, so that today, while Proctor was toiling away in Domestic Security, from which post he would shortly be retired, Battenby, with his monotone voice and safe, well-manicured pair of hands, was in sight of the golden crown. Whisper who dares: because Proctor had spent his time doing the actual work.

'Would you mind awfully, Stewart?'

Proctor obediently opened the door. Enter the tall, redoubtable, wide-striding Teresa, in black power suit, bearing a buff folder with a green diagonal cross splurged across the cover, the Service's most potent symbol for 'keep out'.

'I trust this is going to be all of us, Quentin?' she warned, settling herself unbidden in the other armchair and hauling up her black skirts until it was convenient for her to cross her legs.

'It is,' said Battenby.

'Well, I should bloody well hope so. And I further hope you're not recording this, or anything clever? No one is?'

'Absolutely not.'

'And the janitors haven't left anything on by mistake? Because you never know in this place.'

'I checked,' said Battenby. 'We're not here. Stewart. An update. Are you ready to go?'

'You'd better be, Stewart, because I tell you the wolves are at the door and I'm to get back to them 'ere cockcrow. How's the exquisite Ellen? Leading you a dance, I hope?'

'In fine form, thank you.'

'Well, I'm glad somebody is' – reaching out a long arm and slapping the green-crossed folder on to Battenby's desk. 'Because what we're looking at here is an unparalleled, five-star clusterfuck.'

★

In more leisurely circumstances, Proctor would have kicked off with a portrait of Edward Avon as he had come to know him over the last weeks: simplistic, naive to a fault, damaged from birth, wilful on occasion and surely overblessed with romantic zeal, but quintessentially the loyal Head Agent for all weathers, who had fought the Cold War for us, and went on to the Bosnia thing with the best intentions until a nightmarish episode set him on the wrong path. But this was neither the audience nor the moment for a plea of mitigation. Only the facts could deliver it. He set out to make them do just that:

'I don't know how much you've actually seen of the wild-cat proposals Deborah's think-tank was putting out in the run-up to the second Iraq War, have you, Quentin?'

'Why?' asked Battenby, to Proctor's confusion.

'It was pretty hair-raising stuff, that's all. Informed by our best intelligence, but animated by a political perception, one felt, rather than a viable sense of reality. Simultaneous bombing of Islamic capital cities, gifting of Gaza and South Lebanon to Israel, targeted assassination programmes for heads of state, enormous secret armies of international mercenaries under false flags sowing mayhem across the region in the name of people we didn't like –'

Teresa had heard enough:

'Barking mad moon-gazers, whoever doubted it?' she interrupted impatiently. 'The point is, Stewart, that at exactly the time this dangerous nonsense was being peddled in the wilder corridors of power, Deborah Avon actually came to you and told you, in semi-confidence – whatever that means – that she'd caught her beloved husband sniffing around her strong room, seeking, in her opinion, what he might devour, and you gave her the cold shoulder, and put a milk-and-water note on her file saying she was suffering from ill-health and overwork and seeing reds under the bed. That's going to take some answering at any public enquiry.'

Proctor had prepared himself for this moment and came back gamely enough:

'Florian and Deborah had had an argument about the facts of the matter, Teresa. It was unresolved. Deborah was exhausted, as I wrote, and Florian had been drinking all day –'

'Which you didn't write.'

'There'd been no other evidence from any source that he was spying on his wife or anybody else, and I didn't see myself, as head of Domestic Security, arbitrating in a marital dispute.'

'And it didn't cross your mind to ask yourself why Florian might have been drinking himself stupid right in the middle of Shock & Awe? And now, today, you don't look back and think: that's when he went over?' Teresa demanded.

'No,' Proctor said, letting the answer stand for both questions.

Battenby in his bland voice needed to know how it had come about that the Cheltenham monitors – an object of permanent suspicion to the Service – had fallen down so disastrously on the job:

'And over a period of ten years or more,' he added reproachfully. 'It does seem to me that, on any objective analysis, they do have the larger case to answer, if things ever got that far, wouldn't you say, legally speaking,

Teresa – putting aside entirely any notion of inter-Service rivalry, which we all agree really is a thing of the past?'

'I spoke to their grand wizard this morning and they're out of it. It was our case, they had no brief from us, no context, and no reason to smell a rat. It's the old "What are oranges?" argument. A ton of oranges to a terrorist may mean a ton of hand-grenades, but to a greengrocer it's a ton of oranges. Exactly the same goes with blue-and-white Chinese porcelain. It was dealer to dealer and normal commercial discourse. It's no business of Cheltenham – or it wasn't till last week – who else was listening in, or what a particular trader's ethnic and political affiliations might be. And that's only argument one,' she went on, ignoring Battenby's raised hand, 'because Cheltenham never has one where two will do. Argument two is that the word-codes used, and other equally primitive techniques of obfuscation, were so far below their radar that a child of nine could have cracked them at a glance. Then give us more children of nine, I told him. Half your employees aren't much older, anyway. End of conversation.'

'Have Cheltenham been told anything explicit about the reason behind our enquiry, would you say, Stewart?' Battenby asked, from far away. 'Have we, in briefing them at all, would you say, implied in any way that this might be something of an internal security concern to this Service? Could they have got wind of that, by any chance, do you suppose?'

'Absolutely not,' Proctor replied with confidence. 'We gave them a blanket brief for the whole town, with blue-and-white porcelain flagged, and nothing more. No content, no reason. That's what they're complaining about. We also made a pitch for possibly aberrant phone calls from traders and private houses. Florian is big on using other people's phones. Always pays for his calls, of course, never leaves anyone unhappy. There's a low-end café on the waterfront. It's run by a Pole. Eighteen calls to Gaza in one month for a total of ninety-four minutes.'

'To?' Battenby enquired, touching his computer.

'Mainly to a peace activist named Felix Bankstead, the common-law husband of Florian's former partner Ania,' Proctor replied, grateful for the question, since it gave him a chance to dilute Florian's greater transgressions. 'Florian and Bankstead have been bonding ever since Bosnia. Bankstead edits a bunch of Middle Eastern subscription-only newsletters called *Felicitas*. Florian has been contributing to them for years under a variety of pseudonyms. Polemical stuff, obviously. Bankstead operates as his editor, and cut-out.'

Teresa was not impressed:

'That'll get a good laugh from the tribunal too: pay your fifty quid annual subscription, and read the latest from Britain's spymasters. Mind you, I'll bet he saved his best nuggets for Salma. She got first pick, right, Stewart?'

'And made what use of them precisely, would you say, Stewart, in the large?' Battenby added.

'Distributed them however she thought fit, one assumes,' Proctor said defensively. 'Who to, how, we just don't know yet. But to further her peace efforts, obviously, however misguided that may sound to us.' And, rallying: 'I mean, the fact is, Quentin, that under your strict instructions, we haven't gone into the issue of damage at all. Your feeling was that the moment we turned the Foreign Office analysts loose, whatever cover story we spun them, the cat would be out of the bag. As of now, as far as we know, it's not.'

'Inshallah,' Teresa murmured devoutly.

'Which was how you wanted it played, Quentin.'

'And the broad tone, Stewart, overall' – Battenby, choosing not to hear this – 'of Florian's many anonymous contributions to *Felicitas* and sister publications is what, would you say, for instance?' – in his most speculative, uncommitted voice.

'All pretty much as one would suppose, Vice Chief. America's determination to manage the Middle East at all costs, its habit of launching a new war every time it needs to deal with the effects of the last one it launched. NATO as a leftover Cold War relic doing more harm than good. And poor, toothless, leaderless Britain tagging along behind because it still dreams of greatness and doesn't know what else to dream about,' Proctor said, leaving a brief silence after him – ended by Teresa, who apparently felt the need for a caustic diversion:

'Has Stewart told you what the bugger had the gall to write about this Service in one of his beastly rags?' she demanded of Battenby.

'Not to the best of my knowledge, no,' said Battenby warily.

'According to Florian, writing as John Smith or whoever, the entire Iraq mess is the brainchild of the gallant British Secret Service. Why? Because its two most celebrated spies of all time – T. E. Lawrence and Gertrude Bell – drew up its borders with a ruler and a pencil in a single afternoon. He also had the neck to remind his readers that it was this Service at its most persuasive that talked a power-mad CIA into turfing out the best leader Iran ever had, and thereby precipitated the whole godawful Revolution.'

If this was supposed to be light relief, it had to Proctor's eye the opposite effect on Battenby, who had lapsed into what could be taken for deep thought: that was to say, his limpid blue gaze had turned for inspiration to the blackened window, and a groomed hand was plucking at his lower lip.

'He should have come to us,' he said. 'We'd have listened. We'd have been there for him.'

'Florian should?' Teresa asked incredulously. 'And asked us to change American policy? Then what?'

'It's an historical case. It will never recur and there's no proven damage,' Battenby continued to the window. 'You've told them that?'

'I have, in spades. Whether they're buying it is another matter,' Teresa said.

Proctor had decided to keep a low profile. Had Florian given away the Service's plans or its paralysis? Its sources, or the fact that some part of it had thrown off a long trad- ition of objective advice in favour of a giddy late-life romp through the wild woods of colonial fantasy?

Battenby, finding reasons to consider the whole thing moot: 'And he's deniable. He's not fully British. We can work that up. He was never an established member of this Service, just an occasional employee at best. A bad apple.'

Teresa was not appeased:

'Quentin. For fuck's sake. Did you read Deborah's

obituary in *The Times* on Thursday? I quote: "For the last quarter of a century Debbie, as she was known to her admiring colleagues, was one of Britain's most talented Intelligence officers. Let us hope that one day the full story of her contribution to the nation's weal will be told." Florian was her husband, right? Are you seriously suggesting that if we have him pulled in twenty-four hours after his wife's funeral, the press won't notice?'

Is Battenby suggesting this, Proctor wondered. Is he suggesting anything? Where has he been all this while? Anywhere? Or just sitting on the fence, waiting to see which side pulls harder?

'So for the good of the Service at large,' Battenby said to the window again, as if large puts him at a safe distance, 'what we're looking at here is damage limitation.'

His voice had not risen, but it was no longer so colourless: more, to Proctor's ear, a committee voice in rehearsal. As it continued, the emphasis began to fall into place:

'We shall have to take a very strong line with him indeed. What we're looking at here is a definitive, unqualified confession covering all aspects of his betrayal. Conducted over weeks, or if necessary months, for minimum distribution. Ministers' eyes only. Every single thing he gave her from day one. What she did with it, to his knowledge, and to what end. Without that, there's no prospect of a deal. None. Our terms will have to be' – he seemed reluctant to use the words – 'absolute, draconian and non-negotiable.'

'And so are theirs,' Teresa cut in furiously. 'Whitehall are mad as hornets, in case you don't know. They're not going to be asked to lie their heads off in the morning, and be

caught with their pants round their ankles in the afternoon.
Can we, the Service, guarantee that they won't be reading
"The Adventures of Florian: Volume One" in the *Guardian*
newspaper tomorrow? If we throw the book at Florian,
will it hit him? Because on present performance, it doesn't
look all that likely, if you want their legal opinion. And if
you want mine, this is the best I could get' – opening her
buff folder and brandishing a formal-looking document
with a piece of green ribbon dangling from it – 'wrung out
of them with blood, three hours ago, and there's not a
comma in it they'll alter. If Florian doesn't sign it, all bets
are off.'

★

It is an hour later. If Proctor thinks his cup is full, there is
more good news waiting for him at the front entrance.
Collecting his cellphone from Security, he is greeted by a
text from Ellen sent two hours ago. She is on her way to
Heathrow. The dig, it seems, was not all it was cracked up
to be.

Proctor left London in heavy traffic at nine o'clock that morning driving a Service Ford with his usual caution and wearing a better than ordinary suit. In its inside pocket nestled the long, thin, semi-parchment document that he firmly believed would deliver Edward from the wrath that otherwise awaited him. To himself, and no one else, he thought of it as Edward's stay-out-of-jail card. Now everything was about getting it to Edward, letting him read it, think about it and sign it.

An hour ago, still in Dolphin Square, he had telephoned Silverview and received no reply. At this, he had immediately telephoned Billy, tried and trusted head of the Service's Domestic Surveillance Section, which, ever since the arrival of Deborah's letter, had maintained saturation ground coverage of Florian. For security reasons, Billy had wisely portrayed the operation to his team as a training exercise, and their quarry as a former member of directing staff who would be marking them on performance.

No, said Billy, Florian had not emerged from his house, and was presumably not picking up his phone:

'I should think he's dead to the world, frankly, Stewart. I know I would be. We saw him home yesterday after the funeral. He had his Lily with him till eleven ten. We saw her off to her lover-boy's shop. Florian prowled a bit, we saw his shadow. Three a.m., he put his bedroom light out.'

'And the boys and girls, Billy? Not trying too hard?'

'I tell you, Stewart, I've never been more proud of them than what I am today.'

Proctor had then pondered whether he should send Billy or one of his watchers to rouse Edward, and decided against. Instead, at half past eight, he had rung the book-shop from the car and got Julian, who responded civilly. Was Lily around by any chance?

Lily wasn't. Lily had driven over to Aunt Sophie's in Thorpeness to pick up Sam and then deliver Sophie to Silverview. Was there anything Julian could do to help?

The news came as a secret relief to Proctor, who had not shaken off his guilty feelings after his meeting with Lily in the safe house.

Now he had an idea. It was important to him that Edward should have an early sight of the document by which he was going to have to sign his life away. So, yes, actually, come to think of it, there was something Julian could do to help: did he have a printer handy?

'What for?' Julian demanded, no longer quite so civil.

'Your computer, of course, what do you think?'

'You stole them, remember?'

'Well, do you have a fax machine in the shop?' Proctor persisted, kicking himself for his stupidity.

'We do have a fax machine, Stewart. In the storeroom, yes, we have a fax machine.'

'Who mans it?'

'I can, if that's what you're asking.'

'It is. Can you keep Matthew out of the way while you're standing over it?'

'It can be done.'

'Lily too?' – and in the marked silence – 'I don't want her worrying about this, Julian. She's got enough on her plate. I need to get an urgent document to her father. His eyes only. Something he's got to sign. All very positive and constructive in the circumstances, but it's going to take handling. Are you with me?'

'To a point.'

'I want to send it to you by fax. I want you to put it in an envelope and take it straight to Edward and tell him Stewart Proctor says: "Read closely, I'm on my way, and when and where does he want to meet me so that we can clear this thing up?" Then I want you to call me back on this phone with a one-line answer: time and place.'

He was surprised to find himself addressing Julian as he might any young stripling of the Service, but the boy, he had already decided, was natural Service material.

'What's wrong with emailing Silverview?' Julian objected.

'What's wrong is that Edward on principle does not possess his own computer, Julian, as well you know.'

'And you've stolen Deborah's, I gather.'

'Recovered. It was never her property. And Edward's not picking up his phone, as you will also know. So it's down to you. What's your fax number?'

Neither did it bother Proctor unduly when Julian showed a bit of spirit:

'Are you seriously imagining I'm not going to read this?'

'I'm assuming you will, Julian, and I don't think I mind too much,' he replied airily. 'Just don't wave it around or you'll go to prison for a very long time. You too have signed a document. What's the fax number?'

Proctor then called Antonia, gave her Julian's fax number and instructed her for safety's sake to confirm that it belonged to Lawndsley's Better Books. Assuming it did, she was immediately to send a copy of Edward's stay-out-of-jail card to that number.

Antonia demurred. She needed a signature.

'Then get one from Teresa,' he snapped. 'But do it now.'

Even Proctor was impressed by the homespun nature of these exchanges, given the scale of things to be ironed out, but he had been long enough in the job to know that momentous happenings had a way of acting themselves out on small stages.

By the time he joined the A12 at ten twenty-five, Julian had called him with Edward's answer:

Proctor should come alone. They should meet not at Silverview, which lacked privacy. Edward suggested Orford. If the weather were fine, Edward would be waiting for him at the quayside at three p.m. If not, then in the Shipwreck Café twenty yards away.

'How did he take it?' Proctor asked eagerly.

'Pretty well, by all accounts.'

'By all accounts? You didn't see him?'

'Sophie answered the door. Edward was upstairs in his

bath. He'd had a rough night, she said. I gave her the envelope, she took it upstairs and eventually came down with his answer.'

'Eventually, meaning how long?'

'Ten minutes. Long enough for him to read it a couple of times.'

'How long did it take you to read it?' – joke.

'I didn't, funnily enough.'

Proctor believed him. He would have preferred Julian to have delivered the envelope in person, but, given the fact that Sophie in another life had been Edward's devoted sub-agent, he could hardly have wished for a more reliable intermediary. And he welcomed the idea of Sophie's presence at Silverview at this tricky stage of things. If Edward were under stress, which he could hardly fail to be, she would be a steadying influence.

Pulling into a lay-by, he tapped Orford's postcode into the satnav, examined the map, then called Head Office to tell Battenby of the arrangement. Battenby was away from his desk. Proctor passed a message to his assistant. His next task was to advise Billy of the new arrangements. The team should maintain its watch on the house until Edward left it, at which point a static post should remain in place for his return. The remainder of the team should cover the approaches to Orford, the village square and side exits.

'But I'll need space, Billy, please. He's taking a life decision. No hanging around the quayside buying ice creams, he's up to all that stuff. I want him to know he's got privacy.'

Put differently, he wanted Edward to himself. It was by

now midday. The weather promised well. In three hours, Edward would be waiting for him at the quayside. The more he thought about the coming encounter, the more he relished the prospect. Operationally, Edward was his prize. He had hunted him and cornered him and now he was about to get full disclosure from him, the ultimate: damage, sub-sources if any, modus operandi, known or suspected sympathisers inside the Service – all pretty theoretical, he imagined, since Edward was nothing if not a loner. And – target number one – Edward's reading of Salma's network of end-users, the identity of the people who briefed and debriefed her, if they did, and her network, if she had one.

And when all that was done and dusted, he would ask him frankly, man to man: who are you, Edward – you who have been so many people and pretended to be still others? Who do we find when we've pulled away the layers of disguise? Or were you ever only the sum of your disguises?

And, if that's what you were, how come you endured a loveless marriage, year after year, for the sake of a greater love, by Ania's account at least, that was unlikely ever to be fulfilled?

These were a beginner's questions, of course. And, by asking them, Proctor might be inadvertently revealing himself a little too much for comfort, if only by the keenness of his curiosity. But the chase was over, so what was there to lose? The very idea of a consuming passion bewildered him – let alone of allowing one's life to be conducted by it. Absolute commitment of any sort constituted to his trained mind a grave security threat. The entire ethic of the Service was utterly – he would almost say absolutely – opposed to it, unless, that is, you were talking of manipulating the absolute commitment of an agent you were running.

But Edward was a different creature to any he'd ever come upon, he'd give him that straight off. If you were of a philosophical frame of mind – Proctor largely wasn't – there was a case for saying that Edward was the reality, and Proctor a mere concept, since Edward had endured so many of life's hells and Proctor had only observed a few of them.

What can it have been like, he wondered, to be forged in that furnace of guilt and shame? To know that even if you spend your whole life trying, you'll never get rid of the stain? To invest your all, over and again, only to see it torn away from under you, whether in Poland or – most decisively and literally – in Bosnia?

He remembered Barnie's first report from Paris on Florian, his newest and most exciting 'potential young agent under development', with its references to Florian's 'well-hidden Polish past', as if the Polish past were not his father's but Edward's, something laid on him from birth, and buried from everyone's eyes but his own. And, at the end of the same fulsome paragraph, the conclusion that this same buried past was 'the engine that will drive Florian to work for us against the Communist target in any capacity we care to name'.

And so the engine had indeed driven him – until it was replaced by another engine even more powerful: Salma, tragic widow, mother robbed of her son, secular peace extremist and forever unattainable love.

Intellectually, Proctor could relate to that. And, in their

wide-ranging discussions, he would make sure they put aside the fact that, by any objective standard, Edward had betrayed his country's secrets by spying on his wife, a crime that was worth twenty years of anybody's money.

Did Edward still love the Service despite its many blemishes? He would ask him that too. And probably Edward did, the way we all do.

Did Edward see the Service as the problem rather than the solution? So did Proctor sometimes. Did Edward fear that, in the absence of any coherent British foreign policy, the Service was getting too big for its boots? Well, the thought had crossed Proctor's mind too, he wouldn't mind admitting.

Back to Lily for a moment. The horizon a bit brighter on that front, thank God. Looked as though the poor girl might be tucked up with a really good man. If Jack ever came up with the same good sense that Julian had demonstrated at the farm yesterday, or for that matter just now on the phone, Proctor would be more than content. And if Katie, who herself possessed a solid practical wisdom, among other virtues, managed to land herself with somebody equally level-headed: nothing but applause.

And from there – if they hadn't been with her all the time – his thoughts returned to Ellen, and who or what had persuaded her to change her mind about a sabbatical, and was it really the handsome archaeologist? And, if so, was this her first plunge, or had there been others he didn't know about? Sometimes the whole of marriage was a cover story.

And that, so far as Proctor was ever able to judge

afterwards, was about as far as his thoughts had travelled when he received the unsettling news from Billy that Florian had still not emerged. The drive-time from Silverview to Orford was reckoned at forty minutes minimum. Their appointment was in half an hour.

'Where's his car?' Proctor demanded.

'Still in his drive. Where it's been all night.'

'But he uses cabs, doesn't he? Maybe he had a cab to the back door.'

'Stewart. I've got his front door, his back door, his garden door and his side door, and all his French windows, plus his upstairs windows and his –'

'Is Sophie still there?'

'She hasn't come out.'

'Lily?'

'Up the bookshop. With Sam.'

'Has anyone called at the house since Sophie arrived?'

'One whistling postman, eleven ten, same as every day. Junk mail by the look of it. Had a chat with Sophie on the doorstep, and off.'

'Who's at Orford?'

'I'm in the square, I'm in the pub, I'm at a window in the fish restaurant. I'm not down the quayside because you said not. Do you want me to change that, or stick as is?'

'Stick as is.'

*

Proctor now had a decision to make and he made it quickly. Should he become part of the watch on Silverview, hang around in Billy's van? Or should he assume that Edward had somehow slipped the leash and made it to Orford by some other means? The possibility that he might simply have absconded did not seriously bother him. If a man is about to be given his stay-out-of-jail card, why not stick around to collect it?

Turn left for Orford. Three miles. He turns left.

Single-track road with passing points. The castle appearing on his right side. A white minibus approaches. He pulls over for it. Happy backpackers, he suspects Billy's, probably a changing of the guard. Just stay away from my quayside, all of you.

He enters the square. Central car parking. In the far-left corner, a slip road leading to the quay. He takes it, slowly, admiring the fishermen's cottages either side. A thin trail of pedestrians in both directions, none of them Edward.

The quay lies ahead of him, and, beyond it, small boats, the ness, mist, open sea. To park, or not to park? He parks, ignores the pay-and-display, hurries down a dirty footpath to the quayside.

One small queue of sightseers waiting for the boat tour. One café with an outside deck. People drinking tea. People drinking beer. He looks through the café windows, scans the deck. If you're here, you won't be hiding. You'll be looking out for me.

In the open doorway of a boat house, two local-looking fishermen are varnishing an upturned dinghy.

'You don't happen to have seen a friend of mine around? Avon, Teddy Avon? Comes here quite a bit, I believe.'

Never heard of him, mate.

He returns to the car, calls Billy. Not a dicky-bird, Stewart.

Against all his instincts, Proctor the professional now takes a precautionary measure and rings Antonia his assistant:

'Antonia. How many escape passports did Florian have?'

'Hang on. Four.'

'How many have expired?'

'None.'

'And we haven't stopped them.'

'No.'

'So he kept renewing them, and we did nothing about it. Marvellous. Have them all stopped now, include his legitimate British passport, and get a scream out to all ports, saying detain on sight.'

Call Julian. Should have done it sooner.

*

By the time Proctor entered the gates of Silverview, Julian and Lily had arrived ahead of him as requested. Julian's Land Cruiser was parked in the forecourt and the two of them were on the point of emerging from the house. Lily had her head down and kept it down as she walked past Proctor to the car and sat herself in the passenger seat.

'Edward's not at home,' Julian told Proctor grimly, standing face to face with him. 'We've scoured the house from top to bottom. No note, no nothing. He must have got out in a hurry.'

'How?'

'No idea.'

'Does Lily have any ideas?'

'I wouldn't ask her just now if I were you. But no.'

'What about Sophie?'

'She's in the kitchen,' Julian advised curtly, and climbed into the Land Cruiser beside Lily.

The kitchen vast and gloomy. An ironing board. A smell of washing-day. Sophie, sitting in a wooden armchair with tartan cushions. Fuzzy white hair. The embattled face of a Polish grandmother from the Eastern border.

'It is a mystery,' she said, as if she had found the word only after long thought. 'When I came here, Edvard was normal. He wants tea. I make tea. He wishes a bath. He takes a bath. Then comes Julian. Julian has big letter for Edvard. I push this letter under the door. Maybe for a few minutes he reads this. Is okay, he shouts me. Is okay. Three o'clock okay. Tell Julian. Orford three o'clock. Is okay. After this bath, he takes walk in the garden. Edvard likes to walk. I am in here. I am ironing. I don't see Edvard. Maybe a friend brings a car, takes him away. I do not hear this. Edvard is so sad for his Deborah. He don't speak much. Sophie, he tell to me, I miss my Deborah in my heart. Maybe he go to her grave.'

Parked on a hillside above the town, Proctor steeled himself to call Battenby's office, again got his assistant, told him that Florian had gone missing, had not signed the agreed document, and that Proctor himself had taken the executive decision to cancel all Florian's passports, including his current British passport, and put a watch on all ports.

He was immediately put through to Teresa, who, without equivocation, declared that Edward must be regarded as a criminal on the run, and she proposed to advise the Police and Crown Prosecution services immediately.

'Teresa. Can't you give me a couple more hours, in case he's gone walkabout?' Proctor pleaded.

'Can I fuck. I'm on my way to the Cabinet Office now.'

Proctor again called Billy, this time to order him to deploy his entire team of watchers to scour the countryside – and, yes, call in aerial reconnaissance if he must. If they found Edward, they should restrain him, employing minimal force, but in no circumstances hand him over to the police or anyone else until Proctor has had an opportunity to talk to him.

'It's all too much for him, Billy. He's buying time. He'll come round.'

Did he believe himself? He didn't know. It was by now five in the evening. Dusk was approaching. There was nothing to do but wait. And now and then call Julian in case he or Lily had had word.

*

In Gulliver's coffee bar, the smallest sound was a detonation. After a vigorous session in the playground, Sam lay fast asleep in his buggy. Lily sat on her usual stool at the bar, either head in hands, or staring at her cellphone, willing it to ring. Or going to the window on the off-chance of seeing Edward in his Homburg hat and fawn raincoat sauntering down the street. Twice in the last hour Proctor had rung to ask whether they had news. Now he was ringing a third time.

'Tell him to go to hell,' Lily advised Julian vaguely over her shoulder. In the stress, even bad language had deserted her.

She was about to return to her contemplations when Matthew appeared in the doorway, saying that Little Andy the postman was downstairs in the stockroom, having just finished his round. He needed to speak to Lily on a personal matter.

Taking her cellphone with her, Lily followed Matthew down the stairs. Little Andy, who was six foot four, was wearing jeans instead of his postman's uniform. It crossed Lily's mind – as she told Julian later – that if he had only just finished his round, then he must have done a very quick change. This compounded her sense of foreboding. She also noted that Andy had dispensed with the usual cheerful greetings.

'Only it's about the worst thing we can do, Lily,' he began, starting in the middle rather than at the beginning. 'Carrying an unauthorised passenger. It's curtains for us if we're caught.'

What Andy was really, really worried about, he said, was Mr Avon's state of health – all right, Teddy's – creeping into his van like that, and popping up in the back like a jack-in-the-box and saying, sorry about this, Andy, like it was a joke. If Sophie hadn't had a cup of tea ready for him, Teddy would never have made it into his van in the first place. How he'd managed it at all, the size he was, Andy couldn't imagine.

Julian had by now appeared at Lily's shoulder, and was listening to Andy's story:

'Teddy, I tell him, out. Just out. I'm not saying any more. Then he goes on about how his sister-in-law is coming to Silverview any minute, but that he can't stand the sight of her – no disrespect to your aunt, Lily. Plus he'd lost his car key so what else could he do? Mr Avon, I said. I didn't call him Teddy. I don't care who you are. If you don't get out of my van this minute, I'm pressing my alarm and that'll be your lot and probably mine as well.'

'So did you press it or not?' Lily demanded, sounding to Julian's ear less perturbed than he might have expected.

'It was touch and go, I'll tell you, Lily. All right, Andy, he says. Keep your hair on, I understand entirely and it's quite all right – you know how he is, when he wants to be – just drop me off round the next corner past the garage where nobody can see us and I'll walk it from there and nobody will be the wiser and here's a tenner for you, which I wouldn't take. But he still didn't seem right to me, Lily. Well, I mean, who would, what with Deborah gone like that? Only if this ever gets out –'

'Walk where to?' Lily demanded on the same slightly imperious note.

'He didn't say, Lily, and I didn't get a chance to ask him. He was so fast out of the van, you wouldn't believe. All he told me was, he was getting as far away from your aunt as he could, with due respect. Then afterwards, I went back, didn't I?'

'Back where?' Lily again.

'To have a look at where I'd left him. To see if he was all right. He could have had a fall or something at his age. Only he'd got a lift by then, hadn't he? I mean like within seconds, it must have been.'

'Who with?' Julian this time, while Lily gripped his hand.

'A small Peugeot. Black. Quite clean. You'd be amazed anyone gives lifts round here these days, but they do.'

'Did you see the driver, Andy?' Lily.

'Only from the back. While it was driving away. With Edward up front, which they say is safer if you don't know them.'

'Male or female?'

'You can't see, Lily. Not the way people do their hair these days.'

'What registration?' Julian.

'It wasn't local, I know that. I don't know anyone with a black Peugeot either, not round here. So where's he taken him to? And all because of your aunt, Lily. It didn't make any sense to me at all. And who's to know who picked him up? It could be anyone.'

With lavish thanks and undertakings to contact the police and hospitals only if necessary, and without on any account bringing Andy's name into it, Julian guided him to the door. When he returned upstairs, he discovered Lily, not in Gulliver's, but standing in the bay window of his living room, looking out to sea.

'Just tell me what I'm supposed to do,' he said to her back. 'Do I call Proctor immediately, or just not say anything at all, and hope to God he'll show up here?'

No answer.

'I mean, if he's really in a bad way, maybe it's best to let Proctor find him, and get him some proper help.'

'He won't find him,' she said and, turning to him, revealed an expression so utterly changed – so content, if not radiant – that for a moment he feared for her. 'He's gone to find his Salma,' she said. 'And that's the last secret I'll keep from you.'

Afterword
by Nick Cornwell

I find myself in the position of the cat who not only may look at a king, but is required to say something of substance about him and his work. When I was a teen, that would have been very easy. I was in love with the Smiley versus Karla narrative, and in particular with Michael Jayston's reading of *Tinker Tailor*. I listened to it again and again on my blockish JVC cassette player until I could quote it, down to the cadences: 'I've got a story to tell you. It's all about spies. And if it's true, which I think it is, you boys are going to need a whole new organisation.' I would have told you — and I still might — that David John Moore Cornwell, better known as John le Carré, was not only a superb dad, but also a dazzling and unique storyteller.

The winter of 2020/21 was grim. In early December I found myself in my parents' house in Cornwall looking after my mother, whose cancer was definitely taking itself seriously this time, while my father was in hospital with suspected pneumonia. A few nights later I was crouching at my mother's bedside in the same hospital telling her he hadn't made it. We wept, and I went home alone to stare into the rain over the sea.

I was – am – ridiculously fortunate. When my father died, there was no outstanding business between us; no ill-chosen words or unresolved rows; no doubts and no misgivings. I loved him. He loved me. We knew each other, we were proud of one another. We made space for one another's flaws and we had fun. You can't ask for more.

Except that I'd made a promise. I hadn't done so lightly, but it was back in the metaphorical summer, some time in I don't know what year. We were walking on Hampstead Heath. He was living with cancer too, but it was felt to be the kind you die with rather than from. He asked for a commitment, and I gave it: if he died with a story incomplete on his desk, would I finish it?

I said yes. I cannot imagine saying no. One writer to another, father to son: when I cannot continue, will you carry the flame? Of course, you say yes.

And so, looking out at a wide black ocean on a grim Cornish night, I remembered *Silverview*.

I hadn't read it, but I knew it was there. Not incomplete, but withheld. Reworked, and reworked again. Begun just after *A Delicate Truth*, which I have tended to regard as the perfect distillation of his work – a bravura expression of skill, wisdom, passion and plot. *Silverview*, though, was written, but never signed off. One novel and one promise, both unconsummated.

Was it, then, bad? That can happen to any writer. If it was, could it be rescued? If it could, could it be rescued *by me*? Like my father, I have a capacity for mimicry – but to deploy it at scale, to counterfeit his voice across three hundred pages if the book required it: could I even approach that? Should I?

I read it, and my bewilderment deepened. It was fearsomely good. There were the usual bloopers of the typescript stage – repeated words, technical slips, a very occasional muddy paragraph. But it was more than usually polished for a document not yet in proof, and, like *A Delicate Truth*, it was a kind of perfect reflection on his previous work – a song of experience – and yet fully its own narrative, with its own emotional power and its own concerns. What held him back? What kept it in his desk drawer, to be taken out and redrafted again, and again put away, unsatisfying, until this moment? What, exactly, was I supposed to fix? Should I put eyebrows on this *Mona Lisa*?

On the rare occasions when I'd contemplated this moment and my part in it, I had assumed a three-quarters-finished book, with extensive notes towards an ending, maybe some as yet unincorporated material, so that my job would be a kind of syncretic textual knitting. There was just none of that to be done. An editorial process that was more a clandestine brush pass yielded the version you hold in your hand. It is by any reasonable measure pure le Carré, though you should feel free to blame anything infelicitous on me.

So, again, to the why. Why are you only getting this now?

I have a theory. It is baseless, instinctive and not susceptible of proof. The strict arbiters of verifiability who govern the information circulated by my father's Circus would hang me up by my ears for proposing it. And yet, as Ricky Tarr might, I feel it's true.

There was one line which my father drew more firmly than any other. He would not discuss the aged, yellowed, slightly foxed secrets of his work in the intelligence service. He did not name names, or divulge even to his most dear or most trusted the facts of his time as a secret servant. I know nothing of that period of his life that you cannot read in print in the wider world. He was, despite his departure from SIS in the sixties, loyal to its promises and his own. If there was one thing that offended him deeply, it was the implication, occasionally tossed out by senior officers of the modern community ruffled by his broadsides against the politicisation of intelligence work, that he had betrayed by action or omission his former colleagues. He did not, and, quietly but consistently over many years, they appeared unheralded at his shoulder in bookshops and country lanes, coincidental meetings just long enough to let him know that they knew it.

But *Silverview* does something that no other le Carré novel ever has. It shows a service fragmented: filled with its own political factions, not always kind to those it should cherish, not always very effective or alert, and ultimately not sure, any more, that it can justify itself. In *Silverview*, the spies of Britain have, like many of us, lost their certainty about what the country means, and who we are to ourselves. As with Karla in *Smiley's People*, so here with our own side: it is the humanity of the service that isn't up to the task – and that begins to ask whether the task is worth the cost.

I think he couldn't quite bring himself to say that out loud. I think, knowingly or not, he choked on being the bearer of these truths to – of – from – the institution that gave him a home when he was a lost dog without a collar in the middle of the twentieth century. I think he wrote a wonderful book, but, when he looked at it, he found it cut too close to the bone, and the more he worked on it, the more he refined it, the plainer that became – and here we are.

You can form your own opinion, and it will be as good as mine, but that's what I believe.

My father is in these pages, striving as he always did to tell the truth, spin the yarn, and show you the world.

Welcome to *Silverview*.

Nick Cornwell
June 2021

Nick Cornwell is the youngest son of John le Carré. He writes as Nick Harkaway.

 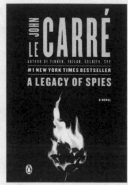